THE PACT

REBELS OF RIDGECREST HIGH

BELLE HARPER

ELEVENTEEN PUBLISHING

BLURB

When we were ten we made a pact.
When we were twelve she moved away.
Now she's sixteen and returned home.

Hunter:
We made the pact when we were ten.
It would be the end of our friendships, we said.
We all agreed. Mila was off limits.
I broke the pact when I was twelve...
I won't break it again.

Jace:
Mila was my best friend, my neighbor and first crush.
But she wasn't just mine.
We made a pact to save our friendships.
Only I broke that pact the day she left.
I won't make that mistake again.

Roman:
Mila was my sunshine, my fighter... my heart.

I broke the pact and she still left.
She destroyed me with that first and last kiss.
Now I fight the monsters alone.
I won't let her in again.

Mila:

Jace, Hunter and Roman.
The four of us were best of friends growing up.
The last time I saw them all, I kissed them goodbye.
I broke their pact before I left, thinking I would never return.
All three believe they were my first kiss.
But I will never kiss and tell.

ONE
HUNTER

My phone goes off while waiting for the guys at the diner. There's a message in the group chat I have with Roman and Jace. Is one of them standing me up?

It's our thing. Every Friday after school is Annie's Diner. Yeah, okay, we're on summer break for a few more days, but still. I don't want them to bail on me. I need this.

I open the message, and my mouth goes dry.

Four words. Just four simple words. But they hold a much greater meaning to the three of us.

Jace: The pact still stands.

Everything is gonna change this year.

TWO
MILA

At the start of summer, I'd had no idea I would exchange one set of problems for another. It wasn't until I got on that plane—well, more like shoved on—that it really sank in.

I'm not the perfect princess Mom wants me to be. She doesn't need me now that she's having her own baby princess with her new husband. No one needs a teenager who is "out of control."

My dad is waiting for me at the airport. Even though I haven't seen him in person in four years, he looks almost just as I remembered. He's tall with a slim, muscular build. His dark hair is shorter, peppered with a few gray hairs now, and his deep blue eyes water at the sight of me. He has this amazing smile, and when I see it, I burst into tears as I run and hug him tight, like I'm still a little girl. I can't help it. He has always been my rock. My real parent.

My mom on the other hand…she's never wanted this life and has made it clear that I wasn't planned. I was an accident. She'd had dreams and, apparently, I'd ruined them by existing. Dad wasn't part of those dreams either.

My mother not only broke my father's heart when she'd cheated on him. She'd ruined him in the most brutal way. By taking the only thing he wanted—me.

She hadn't cared who she destroyed in the process. She'd wanted the dream life. Apparently, that had included me playing happy family with her, her new husband, and his kid in New York. I'd only been twelve, but I'd thought she had forgotten I existed until then. I was forced to move across the country, away from my dad. My friends.

My mother is a selfish bitch who only thinks of herself. There's no way to sugarcoat it. She cheated on my father with a first-class passenger. Yeah, my mother, the flight attendant, joined the mile high club and decided her life was more interesting with Mr. New York City. She packed her bags and left us.

It had been fine with me. I barely saw her, and when I did, it wasn't a loving relationship. If anything, she'd used me to make herself look like this amazing mother figure to her friends. I'd been happy when she left me with my dad. He was my everything.

But, a few months later, she'd returned and took my father to court for full custody. He wasn't working full time, so the judge determined he couldn't support me on his income.

It wasn't his fault. He worked part time to take care of me while my mother had her dream career. Dad only worked the hours I was at school. He was there to pick me up every day. My mom never picked me up, not even once. She spent her days off drinking wine with her friends instead.

Dad couldn't fight her or the new husband's money. He tried. I know he did. I'd had no choice but to live with mom and my stepfather in New York and play happy family with her, Malcolm Senior, and his son—Malcolm Junior, my stepbrother.

He was named after his dad, but he goes by Junior. I mostly call him Malcolm just to piss him off. The rest of the time, I call him asshole. *Never Junior.* He's a year older than me and stays at the academy he attends, so I only see him a few times a year when he isn't at school or with his mom.

Last week had been the exception. He came back to town for the summer before college and didn't tell anyone he was staying at the apartment. Mom and Malcolm were in Paris, celebrating the pregnancy, you know, like regular people do when they find out they are having a baby. *Pompous assholes.* But it gave me time away from them, so I didn't care.

Junior invited his academy friends over and partied. So, I joined them. When in Rome and all that. Only, the days blended into each other. Drugs and alcohol were passed around like candy. I might have dabbled a little— okay, more than a little—in what was on offer. I was angry with my mom. Angry at the world.

I was having a moment and enjoying it.

I hadn't known Mom and Malcolm would return to the apartment so soon. What had felt like two days of partying had actually been seven.

Let's just say, they weren't happy. *With me.* Junior is a good kid. I'm the troubled one. My grades are bad, I get into trouble at school, and I hang out with the "wrong crowd."

I'm the "bad influence" on Junior, taking advantage of him with my "feminine wiles." And I had to go.

Who the fuck uses the term *feminine wiles* these days?

My old-as-hell stepfather, that's who. Really showing his age with that one. He's in his late sixties, while my mom is still young at thirty-five.

She had me at eighteen. Nothing like a high school graduation party and hooking up with the star football player with a college scholarship. Then finding out you're pregnant just before you start college. Yep, I'd heard that story one too many times.

Dad gave up his scholarship to attend a local college to support Mom and me. She never mentions that in her sob story. That he gave up his dream. I asked him about that, but he told me it was his dream to be a father, and football was always second. That I made his dreams come true. My parents are polar opposites of each other.

When Mom told me I was moving back with my father permanently, I didn't get upset. That didn't sound like a punishment to me at all. It is what I have wanted for the last four years.

"It's bad for the baby, Malcolm. She has to leave now." She'd put on her stupid pouty face and batted her eyelashes at him. *"She's taking advantage of Junior, and we have to think of our baby now. Our baby and Junior come first."*

That still stings, even though I know she's like that. She doesn't want me but doesn't want my dad to have me either. She's a petty, hurtful bitch.

"I won't have a girl like you ruining the reputation of my son. Dragging our name down with your indecent behavior."

Funny how it was me who took Junior down. I wasn't the one naked, a joint hanging from my lips, pounding into the girl bent over the back of the couch when they walked into the apartment.

I was in the kitchen, pouring myself a glass of water,

trying to rid myself of the pounding headache. Or maybe the pounding was just coming from Junior and the girl.

I hadn't gotten a chance to sober up when I saw Mom and Malcolm, and I'd refused to defend myself when their idea of a punishment was my dream come true. Let them think I was this horrible person. I bet, even if I hadn't been there, it still would have been my fault. I was going home to my dad, and that was all that mattered to me.

They packed two suitcases full of my clothes, dragging my half-hungover ass into a black town car. At the airport, Mom shoved the ticket into my hand as Malcolm Senior stood there, rubbing her back. Comforting his poor wife—that's what it would have looked like to the outside world. A mother upset her daughter was leaving and the supportive husband there to comfort her. Always an actress, my mother. Putting on the right face and playing the part she wants others to see.

Only I see the real her. She's ugly inside. Black and rotten to the core.

"You're a whore, Mila," she'd hissed quietly into my ear as she grabbed my wrist tightly, digging her perfect French manicure into my skin.

Pulling back, she glanced behind me, where the staff waited for me to board, and dabbed under her eye with her finger.

I rolled my eyes, so glad to be done with her theatrics. Looking her in the eye, I grinned wickedly. "I learned from the best, Mother. Thought you would be proud."

Dad pulls into the driveway of my childhood home. It looks the same as it did the day I left. The shrubs have grown, but apart from that, it's the same. White with a blue door. My heart swells at the sight. I didn't know I'd be this emotional at seeing the house. But I am. This is my home.

I'm finally home.

I get out of the truck and take a deep breath of fresh air. I absorb the sounds of birds and a lawn mower. I love the smell of freshly cut grass. This is the place I should have been for the last four years. If only my mom had gotten knocked up by Malcolm years ago, she wouldn't have bothered with me, and I would have stayed here with Dad.

"I'll grab your bags." Dad smiles as he rounds his old truck. The same faded blue truck he bought when he was seventeen. He's always loved it, even though it smells a little funky and is loud as hell. It's just as I remembered it. Like nothing has changed at all.

I hear a door slamming. I turn to the left, and that's when I see him. A much older version of my childhood best friend.

Jace Montero.

Wow.

Like, holy fucking shit.

He'd grown up. He's over six feet, maybe six-three. The dark brown hair he used to keep short is longer on top. Styled all messy, it looks good on him. He wears a white tee that accentuates his olive skin. The fabric clings to his skin, displaying the outline of a perfect set of abs.

Dang.

Growing up, Jace was scrawny and shorter than most

kids our age. He was always shorter than me. Five gold stars to puberty.

Puberty shafted me in height. I'm five-five. Okay, that's a lie, but let me think I'm that tall. I haven't really grown in four years, so of course, Jace is taller. Most people are.

His steps falter as he notices me. His eyes meet mine and he freezes, like he's seen a ghost. I guess, in some ways, I am one. Been gone four long years without a word. I could have been dead or in jail. But I guess Dad would have mentioned my passing.

My heart speeds up as he stares at me. God, I hadn't realized how much I'd missed him. He looks away and he quickly makes his way to the driver's door of a shiny black SUV in the driveway. When he looks up at me again, I take my chance—I smile and wave.

At least I have old friends here. I might not have spoken to them in four years, but I'd known Jace for twelve years before I left. I don't have to worry about being the new kid next week at school, just the old kid returning.

Jace turns and climbs into his car, ignoring me. My heart sinks.

To be honest, it was what I'd expected from Jace and what I deserve. A positive reunion would have been nice, but I hadn't been holding my breath for one. When I left here, I couldn't handle the idea of seeing how happy my friends were. Couldn't handle their happy smiles during video chats. While they had each other, I had no one. I spent the first few weeks crying to my mom to let me come back home. I was missing everything.

So, for the past four years, I haven't spoken to any of them. I cut all ties with this life. The only connection I had was my dad, who I spoke to twice a week. Mostly about movies, football, his new job, and what I was doing in school. He never mentioned the guys. He must have known I didn't want to talk about them.

I hadn't known what to expect when I got back here. There hasn't been a lot of time to process everything.

It's not like I can take back the last four years like they didn't happen.

They did.

I clutch my hands together, my left thumb brushing over the palm of the right. Over the scar that was left there the last time we were all together. The scar I know is on Jace's palm too.

The one thing that still connects us.

THREE
JACE

She's back. *Fuck.*

Mila Hart had been my neighbor since birth. We grew up together. Our parents became good friends. Having dinner at each other's houses every week was normal to me. Her dad, James, coached our flag football team right up until she left.

Mila wasn't only my neighbor. She was my first and best friend for twelve years.

She wasn't given a choice in leaving. She'd wanted to stay. I hated her mom for taking her away. I'd known things would be different with her being so far from us, but the distance wasn't the problem. Mila was.

I called her every day. And every call and message that went unanswered was like a dagger to my heart. It only took her two weeks in New York to forget about us.

When she left, she really left us. Nothing, not one word to any of us, in four years.

Now she's standing there, beside her father's truck, looking like a womanly version of the girl I once knew. Her hand on hip with her head cocked to the side told me it was Mila instantly. She has that kind of attitude about her. Sassy and confident, my mom would always describe Mila.

Her blonde hair is longer and hangs in waves over her shoulders. Her black, ripped skinny jeans and tight red tank top show me she's not the little girl I once remembered. She stands there looking like some model off a runway.

But she isn't a model. She's the girl next door, and she's always been beautiful no matter what she wears. *Fuck…*

She smiles and waves at me, like the last four years she wasn't here don't mean a thing.

Mila isn't my best friend anymore. If anything, she broke me when she stopped taking my calls. I won't tell her that. She messed up, and if she thinks I'll forget about it and wave back—that I'll tell her, "It's good to see you"—she's delusional.

I'm angry with her. I didn't realize that until I saw her. *Fuck.*

I slam my fist on my steering wheel. I don't want anything to do with her. I hope she returns to where she came from. But with school starting Monday, I have a feeling she isn't here just for the weekend to visit her dad.

She hasn't been to visit her dad once in all these years. I asked him about her for months after she stopped talking to me, thinking maybe her phone was broken or her mom had grounded her. But he spoke to her all the time. That's how I knew she didn't want to speak to me.

The others need to know she's back. I wasn't the only one who missed her when she left. When she cut me off, she cut us all off. I don't know how they'll feel about her returning. I can't let her get between us again.

She almost broke us apart when we were ten and all

had a little crush on her. Now we're grown and horny as fuck all the time. The pact needs to stand more than ever. She has the power to destroy us, and I can't let that happen.

When we were ten, Roman and Hunter fell for her. Just like I did. It wasn't hard with a girl like Mila. She was everything. She played football with us in Hunter's backyard, tackling all of us, getting mud and bruises on her body. She would claim she was the knight of the castle, wearing a pink tutu and attacking us with her plastic sword.

"It isn't a crush, I love her," Hunter told us.

Roman pushed him over. "I'm gonna marry her. You can't love her."

I was worried she would pick one of them, and we wouldn't be friends anymore. There would be Mila and the one she chose, the two losers left to watch, heartbroken. I wouldn't be one of the losers. She was mine first. I loved her first. I was going to marry her.

I told them we had to make a pact.

"We can't all love her and still all be friends when she picks one of us. It will tear us apart. Friendship is all we need. So, we make a pact now. No one can love or marry Mila. *Ever*. No one can break the pact. It's for life."

We all spit into our palms and shook hands. We'd seen it in a movie, and we did it whenever something was "for life." The pact was done. Sealed in our spit. Except, I crossed my fingers with my other hand when I made that pact. Mila, she was mine. I was going to keep her forever.

But now that she was back, I didn't want her. I couldn't let Roman or Hunter have her either. It would break us apart worse than ever.

Roman took it the hardest when she left. He's still

fucked up now. Mila had filled a hole for him that Hunter and I couldn't. We'd tried to help him, but he spiraled into a deep, dark depression. He's still in that dark place, but he's better than before. I'm worried her reappearance might make him spiral again.

I'm so angry with her. What she did to me, to Hunter, and especially Roman. She'd known he needed her more than any of us, and she left him to the wolves.

I bring up the group chat on my phone, anger bubbling within me.

Jace: The pact still stands.

I throw my phone onto the passenger seat, my foot on the gas as I tear backwards out of my driveway. I throw my car into drive and dare myself not to look back at her.

I grip the wheel tightly. I won't cave for her. I won't look at her. She means nothing to me, and I don't need her shit in my life. I'm happy without her. At the last second, my eyes dart to my rearview mirror. She watches me just as I watch her.

Fuck. I'm fucked.

"Are you sure it's her? Mila? Mila Hart is back?"

Hunter hunches closer to me in our booth at Annie's Diner. Meanwhile, Roman arches back, resting his head on the wall behind him, his expression unchanged at the news of Mila's return. But I know he's turning shit over in his mind. Hunter, on the other hand, is more interested in Mila being back than I thought he would be.

"Yes, that's what I said five minutes ago. It's not a big deal. Why do you keep repeating yourself?"

He throws a few fries in his mouth and chews while he nods. More to himself than me. I fight the urge to roll my eyes.

"Because…out of nowhere, you text us that the pact still stands. Then, you come in here and tell us she's returned home. That's a big deal."

"Hey, Jace." Britney slides in beside me. I put my arm around her shoulder, and she gives a small girlish giggle.

We've been dating on and off for the past year. Mostly off. But I keep going back. I guess it's easy because she knows what I like. And I don't mean football or food. She knows how to suck my cock just right. Yeah, I'm an asshole.

"But, like, how does she look? You won't tell us anything. Throw a guy a bone here. Is she hot now? Fuck, I bet she's all grown up and shit and that's why you're not telling us, so you can get to her first. The pact stands for you too, Jace."

I roll my eyes at Hunter, not wanting to talk about Mila. Even now, I'm getting angry again thinking of all the years she ignored me. My jaw ticks at the thought of her being back and Hunter wanting to know how she looks.

She looks hot. Hell, if it wasn't Mila, I would have been over there trying to get her number. Britney perks up; she heard what Hunter said.

"Who's hot? Who can you get first?" She sits back and glares at me.

Like I was cheating for even knowing someone who could be hot. This is why we broke up more than anything. If a girl even looked my way, she had a melt-down that I was flirting or cheating. I would break up with her permanently, but when she comes back to apologize each time, it is on her knees. How can I say no to that?

"Mila Hart." Hunter takes a bite of his burger. The melted cheese runs down his fingers as he hides a grin, knowing what he just did.

"Fucker," I mumble under my breath at him.

"What are you doing looking at her? Doesn't she live, like, a million miles away?" she screeches.

My grip on her neck is tight—it won't hurt her, but it acts like a warning as I pull her in close until our foreheads are touching. "We talked about this at the start of summer. I will break it off, and permanently this time, if you do this shit. I'm not cheating. The possessive, jealous shit from you needs to stop now."

She bats her lashes at me. I fight the urge to roll my eyes and push her away just for drama's sake, but fuck, I wish she wasn't here right now. I need space, time to think, but she isn't gonna leave anytime soon.

"Sorry, Jace. I won't do that again, I promise."

She kisses the corner of my mouth, but I pull away before she can go any further. I'm not in the right frame of mind to be kissing Britney right now. Not when I wish I was kissing someone else and hating myself for it.

I find Roman watching me. He isn't stupid; he would have seen my reaction to Britney and read into it. Fuck, do I care? *No. Yes.* I don't know.

I feel like screaming and hitting something.

He breaks eye contact with me first as he gazes out the window, looking worn down. More so than usual. I'd known her return would affect him. The question is—how badly?

"You think she will go to Ridgecrest High or Lakeview Prep?"

I want this conversation to end, but I can tell Hunter won't drop it.

"No idea, I didn't talk to her. Not gonna, either. She didn't speak to us for four years. Why would I start talking to her now?" But even I know that's a lie.

"I hope she comes to Ridgecrest," Hunter continues.

"Yeah, well, her dad is working over at Lakeview Prep, so he would have some type of a teacher discount, I would think. Makes more sense for her to go there, anyway."

"Nah, man, you remember when we were kids, and we were all gonna go to Ridgecrest High. We thought it was the coolest place ever. We were gonna run the halls."

I let out a snort. We had thought it was cool. It isn't. But we'd been right about one thing—we do run the halls.

It's easy when you're the quarterback for Ridgecrest Rebels. Roman is my fullback, and Hunter—with his shit-eating grin—is my wide receiver. And this is gonna be our year. We are juniors but we had proven that we were the best.

Plus, they don't call us the Rebels for nothing. We get up to a lot of trouble.

"We should throw a party before your parents get back," Hunter suggests.

"Yeah, okay, but I gotta talk to Grady first. Make sure he's onboard and shit. I don't want him telling my parents. But it's low key, okay? Just a few guys from the team and some girls." I turn to Roman. "Are you cool with getting beer?"

He doesn't move or even blink.

"Roman?"

His eyes find mine, and he raises a brow.

"Beers? You think you could grab us some for the party tomorrow night?"

He nods and shifts his weight, snagging a fry off Hunter's plate. Hunter always orders extra fries, knowing

Roman will eat them. Growing up, he wasn't the type of guy to ask for food when he was hungry, or accept you buying him any, but Hunter always ordered "too much," and Roman couldn't let it go to waste.

Roman knows Hunter could never finish them. He's told him to stop over-ordering time and time again. But Hunter keeps on ordering extra. This has been going on for three years now. Roman doesn't wait for Hunter to offer them anymore, he starts eating them as soon as the plate hits the table. It's something we don't talk about. It's just how we are.

When Roman speaks, you listen. He doesn't sit around and talk shit like Hunter and I do. He's quiet but not timid or anything. He'll tell you straight to your face what he thinks of you. But he doesn't speak unless there's something worth saying.

He doesn't have any other real friends but me and Hunter. Growing up, Mila was the closest friend Roman ever had. When she left, he spoke less, he grew quieter. And, for a while, he didn't come to school. We had to go over to his place and drag him to school. Our moms helped a lot with that too. Made sure he was clothed and fed. His dad was a grade-A asshole, through and through. My mom wanted to report him to child services, but Roman would say, "I would rather live with the devil, than a devil wearing angel's clothes." Mom didn't call them after that, but she always made sure he was safe.

Mila used to be the one to protect him, keep him safe. He talked to her, he even smiled with her and picked flowers—not that he would admit that. I haven't seen him smile in four years. I'm not sure if he's capable of smiling anymore. And this is why Mila can't come back into our lives. I need to protect Roman. She hasn't been here. She won't understand how bad he got and what we've done to get him here today.

"I can get the girls together, and we'll all be there."

I look back at Britney, raising my brow. "What girls?" I ask, confused.

"For the party, silly."

Caught up again in thoughts of Mila, I'd almost forgotten about the party we just organized moments before.

Britney rubs my arm and lean in close, her tits pressing against my side. "It's like you zoned out there, baby."

I clench my jaw at her pet name for me—I hate it.

But I hate Mila Hart more.

FOUR
MILA

My sudden return has my dad scrambling to get everything organized for me. He was literally given hours before I rocked up here. Same as me. But he needs to enroll me in school, and he's talking about getting me a car, mumbling about the models he thinks would be safe but cheap to run. I'm worried a car would be too much for my dad's budget. I don't need a car. Yeah, I can drive, I made sure of that, but I can catch the bus. I really don't care. I'm happy to just be home.

"Your room is the same. I haven't touched it since you left. We can go get you a bigger bed, if you want?"

I shrug. "I'm only one person, Dad. I don't need a bigger bed."

Walking into the house is like walking into a memory of a happier time. It looks the exact same as the day I left. Even though I've been gone all these years, it's like I just came back from a short trip. Not four years.

It even smells the same. The scent of safe, happy memories. Like I can finally breathe and relax for the first time since stepping on that plane today.

I notice one change—the photos of my parents are missing, replaced by photos of me that I'd sent Dad via email. He'd printed them off and put them into frames. My chest feels tight, and my eyes start to water. The lump in my throat thickens, and I know I'm going to cry. Again.

I imagine Dad having a life here all these years without me. I'd missed him so much. Forcibly, I swallow my emotions and plaster on a smile.

"Do I get to meet Kate?" I spin and face him.

My dad has been dating a woman for the past few months, and from the way his voice changes when he speaks about her, he's truly happy and in love with her.

He puts my suitcases down, appearing uncomfortable. "Oh, I wasn't sure if you'd want to just yet." He scratches the back of his head, and is that a blush? Is my dad blushing?

"Why wouldn't I? She makes you happy, and I want to meet her."

All I know about her is that she's divorced and has two kids, a boy and a girl. They met at school, where he works as the assistant football coach. Her kids are students there. They must come from money, because Lakeview Prep isn't cheap.

"I usually go over to dinner most nights, but I canceled when I heard you were coming so we could spend some time together. I thought you might want to settle in first before I introduced you."

My feet began moving before my brain could register what I was doing. I wrap my arms around Dad's waist and hug him tight.

"You are amazing, Dad, but I want to meet her. Her kids. You don't need to cancel. We can still go, if you want."

I hope her kids are better than Malcolm Junior. I'm unsure how well off they are, so I kinda want to get this over with sooner. Just in case they're pricks. I know the boy is my age; he plays for the football team at Lakeview Prep. I can't remember his name, though. The girl is fourteen, and her name is Madison.

Dad pulls out his phone then glances up at me. "Are you sure you don't want to stay in and get settled? We could order pizza and watch an old football game or a movie?"

I shake my head. "Nope," I reply, popping the p. "I think it would be good to meet them today."

"Okay, but first I need to speak to the school about getting you enrolled. I'm not impressed about your grades since you've been gone, but I'm sure we can convince Mr. Key they'll only improve now that you're back home."

After witnessing the warm welcome Jace gave me, if I was a normal person, I would want to avoid him and go to Lakeview Prep. I know he goes to Ridgecrest High. He wouldn't have left Roman behind to go to some pompous prep school. Even Hunter, whose parents are loaded, promised to never separate us. He'd planned to attend Ridgecrest with us. Only, I never got there. I was dragged away before I could.

But, even now, I still want to go there. I want to see my old friends. I'm hoping for a warmer welcome from Hunter. Roman, I won't hold my breath. I'd known cutting him off would be the end of what we'd built for all those years, and I would have to start over with him. I'd broken his trust, and that will be a long road back. One I'm determined to walk. No matter what he throws at me.

"I want to go to Ridgecrest, Dad. All my old friends are there."

He looks down at me, furrowing his brow. "You don't want to come to Lakeview? They have an amazing art program. I know you still like art."

I shake my head. "I don't want to go there. I never planned on being there when I was younger, and I really want to be at Ridgecrest."

Dad clears his throat. "Okay, I will call and see if I can get you transferred there. Go up to your room and settle in while I make some calls."

I walk up the stairs, noticing all the old photos still hanging on the wall. Except one—my parents' wedding picture. It's been replaced by a photo of my grandparents. My dad lost them both when he was eighteen. I never got to meet them, but my middle name is June, after my grandmother. I touch the glass over her face. She was beautiful.

I continued up, the top stair squeaking, and I smile. Pressing it with my toe, it squeaks again. Dad never fixed it. I was really back.

My bedroom is at the opposite end of the hallway to Dad's. The door is closed, and when I turn the handle and look inside, it's dark. It smells dusty too. Like once I left, he'd closed the door and had never come back in here.

I move to the blind and open it, the sunlight streaming through. Turning, I put my hands on my hips as I survey the room. Same bed, same sheets. My nightstand has a thin coating of dust, and my pink alarm clock is flashing at me, needing to be reset. I open my closet and find all my old clothes from when I was twelve. My pink skateboard and helmet are hiding in there too. I pull the skateboard out and flip it over in my hands. I wasn't very good at it, but I'd still tried to keep up with the boys. It was more Roman's thing.

"Mila," Dad calls out, and I spin to see him entering my room. "I just got off the phone with Ridgecrest. You can start Monday with everyone. We just have to go in and get everything settled in the morning."

I let out a deep sigh of relief, glad I wasn't going to a prep school. It isn't my style. I'd already been at a pompous private schools for the past four years. I have zero intention of going back to that.

"Thanks, Dad." I put the skateboard down and move over to my single bed. "I think I might need to wash these sheets. They haven't been changed in four years, and they're a little dusty."

I tap my palm down in the middle of the purple comforter, and dust particles rise up and dance in the sunlight. He chuckles, and I do too, until I sneeze. Even then, I can't keep the smile off my face.

Studying Dad, I can't help but notice the fine lines along his eyes and mouth. He's aged since I left, but he still looks young and handsome.

"I'm just so happy to have you back, Mila. This"—he waves his hand at me and the room—"back again. Under my roof and with me."

I hug him, swallowing the lump forming again. I can't seem to keep my emotions at bay. "Me too, Dad. I won't go back."

That's a promise.

Dad leaves me to wash the bedding and let me unpack. He gave me some bags to fill with old clothes in my closet that don't fit anymore and supplies for cleaning. He'd really left my room untouched.

I even find my Halloween candy stash that are years past their expiration.

Needing some fresh air, I open the window, and the smell of the freshly cut grass from the neighbor behind pours in. I hear a voice calling out and laughing. I peer into the yard of Jace Montero and see his older brother Grady there with another guy. They're topless, lounging on outdoor chairs, drinking beer and laughing.

My heart races at the sight of Grady. I might have had a little crush on him growing up. Jace and I used to drive him crazy. Back then, we'd found it funny. Now, I realize he must have considered me an annoying little sister. He'd called me that once and, like a bucket of cold water, had doused all the flames of the girlish crush I'd had on him.

He has filled out…the washboard abs and the tan he's rocking have my body very aware he has only gotten better with age. I can see his jaw has sharpened too and those full lips of his are even more kissable than ever.

I lean out my window, preparing to say hello. But I'm distracted by the walkie-talkie on the windowsill. My parents and Jace's gave them to us for Christmas when we were eight. Mine is exactly where I used to leave it each night, in case Jace wanted to talk to me. Our houses are a mirror of each other. My bedroom looks out over the side of his yard, as does Jace's room with mine.

I look toward his window, finding the blinds drawn. Clicking the button on the walkie-talkie, it comes to life. I smile at the white noise. It reminds me of the last Halloween we were together and Jace slept over.

• • •

"Shh, he might hear us," Jace warns as I let a giggle slip. We're hiding under my windowsill.

"How is he gonna hear us when we are in my house, silly? Plus, he's looking for the candy stash we said we left in there." I raise my brows at Jace, and he just shakes his head with a huge grin.

I grab a piece of candy corn from the bag we got from trick-or-treating earlier and throw it at Jace. He catches it and pops it into his mouth with a grin.

Grady said he was "too old" to trick or treat, but he wants our candy. He's barely a year older than us. I didn't see how that was too old. But we don't want to share it with him when we did all the hard work.

We'd put all our candy into one big bag, like we do every year. We share it and have a sleepover. There are flavors I don't like but Jace does, and some he hates and I think are the best. So, it makes sense to combine it and eat it all together.

"Here, give it to me." He reaches out with his palm open, and I give him the walkie-talkie and turn around.

My fingers grip tightly to the edge of the windowsill as I peek up to see if Grady is still in Jace's room. "He's still there, looking. He's going into the closet. Wait...wait...do it...now."

I put my fist to my mouth, trying to hold myself together as Jace makes a creepy sound into the walkie-talkie, knowing it'll broadcast to the one hiding in his closet.

Grady jumps and runs out of Jace's room. We burst into laughter until our tummies hurt. That was the best. We got Grady so good. Jace sits up next to me now, and we both look into his room, waiting to see if Grady comes back.

It only takes a few minutes before Grady storms back into the room. He looks at us and points. He isn't happy.

"Busted," Jace and I say at the same time, and we burst into giggles.

"You two," Dad says at my bedroom door, startling us. We quickly turn and sit up straight, pretending we weren't doing anything. "No more candy; it's time for bed. And stop scaring Grady or I will confiscate the walkie-talkie."

Our mouths drop open. We weren't good at pretending at all. Dad moves to close my door, but he winks at us just before closing it. We look at each other, brows raised, before bursting into another round of giggles.

I smile to myself. It's one of my favorite memories. I have a lot, but that night was particularly fun. The next day, not so much. Grady told me I was like an annoying sister that he didn't have and didn't want.

With those few words, my crush disappeared in the blink of an eye.

I move back inside the room and turn away from the window. Suddenly, I have no desire to see Grady. I'm worried he'll react like Jace did, and I don't think I can handle rejection twice in an hour.

I glance back at my dusty, disheveled room.

This was gonna be a long afternoon.

FIVE
MILA

Turns out, partying and lack of sleep over seven days catches up to you, and even a small nap on the plane won't save you from that huge crash you knew was coming but hoped wouldn't. Dad said I was talking in circles when he found me lying on my freshly made bed and wanted to let me rest. So, he went to dinner without me and let me sleep it off.

I slept all night and all day. He let me know he had an emergency coaches' meeting at five, and he wasn't sure when he would return. He told me he was sorry and to not wait up for him, promising we would do something together tomorrow before school on Monday. I shooed him away, told him his job is important and I still had some stuff I needed to unpack.

But now it's after nine and I'm wired...too awake and nothing to do. I tried Netflix. There's only so much I haven't watched, and I'm not interested in restarting anything.

I pull out an old book I found in the closet, but it isn't

holding my interest. It isn't the book—it's me. More than anything, I want the last four years to have never existed. I want to go next door and hang out with Jace and play his Xbox with him. Like we used to.

I want to ride my bike down to the lake and use the rope swing, teasing Hunter that he's chicken for not jumping in. I want to pick daisies with Roman, not that he would ever tell anyone. That had been our thing after his mom died. She'd loved daisies, and we would pick them and place them on her headstone in the cemetery.

I miss my old friends, my old life here. I want it back, and I have no idea where to start.

I hear the thumping of a bass outside. Peering out my bedroom window, I spot a few people I recognize from elementary school. There's a party next door. We never used to have parties like that. And now Jace is throwing one, knowing I'm here and intentionally not inviting me.

It's like Jace wrote me completely off. All the memories of us, how we used to be, are flooding back now I have returned. And I've been feeling more emotions in the last twenty-four hours than I had in the last four years.

D*addy is driving Jace, Grady, and me to school today. It's the same as every other school day, but today, Hunter, our friend from last year, is waiting for us. I'm really excited to see him again after summer.*

"I want to walk you both in," Daddy tells us again.

Grady had already jumped out the car. He was a second grader now and tall like me. He said I was smart enough to be a second grader, and I got butterflies when he said that. Daddy calls me smart all the time, but he has to say nice things, he is my daddy. It was different when Grady said it, it felt...real.

"Daddy, no, stay in the car." I huff and roll my eyes at him. Then I give him my best smile, begging him with my eyes to not come in. I want to do this by myself. "I'm a big girl now."

"Okay...I will be back later, you two first graders. Have fun." He winks at us as I jump up and wrap my arms around his neck and kiss his nose.

"Love you, Daddy."

Daddy was the best. We'd told him we were big kids now and didn't need him to walk us into school. We know what we have to do. We're first graders now.

Jace and I laugh as we run onto the school grounds. As I turn to see his smiling face, I'm bumped hard by a big kid and almost fall over.

"Watch where you're going, dweeb," a tall, mean girl snarls at me.

Jace grabs my hand and pulls me to him, putting me behind his back and facing off with the tall girl. "You pushed my friend. Apologize to her," he demands.

Tall, mean girl and her friends laugh at him. "The little baby wants me to apologize. Go change his diaper, dweeb. He's just a little baby." She starts to make crying baby sounds.

I'm angry—how dare she. No one laughs at my Jace and gets away with it.

He's small for a first grader, but I am a whole head taller than Jace and closer in height to this girl than he is. I love that he wants to protect me, but I'll protect him too.

"Don't laugh at him. You're rude. You pushed me and called me a dweeb. I'm not a dweeb, you are. And your hair looks bad." I add that last part in hopes of hurting her feelings back.

She shoves me, and I stumble back.

I hear Hunter calling out to me, and I turn around to see his worried expression as he runs up to us. The tall, mean girl chooses that moment to shove into me from the back. My hands automatically come out in front to catch my fall, but they slide down in the dirt, and my whole body feels like it's surfing the ground, until I come to a stop.

The pain in my hands causes a tear to form in my eye, but I won't cry. I'm not a crier. I twist to see her friends have taken a step back and aren't laughing anymore. They look concerned. But the tall, mean girl is pointing at me and laughing, not caring that my pretty dress is all dirty and torn.

I roll over and look at my knees. They're bleeding like my hands and there is dirt and stones in the wounds. My throat gets tight, but I won't cry. Not yet.

Jace is by my side and Hunter is calling out for a teacher to come help while he stands between me and the mean girl. Protecting me from her.

Tall, mean girl shoves Hunter next, and something snaps inside me, my knees and hands forgotten. I crouch low, just as Daddy showed me in the backyard. He loves football so much, and we watch it together all the time. I tell him when I grow up, I'm going to "tackle boys." He always chuckles but teaches me every weekend in our yard how to play football.

Hunter must see the look in my eyes because he moves away as my feet press hard into the dirt. I keep my body low as I charge at her. Her expression remains the same, except the widening of her eyes right before I wrap my arms around her legs and take her down. Hard.

I sit back and watch her sprawled out on the ground beneath me. Her face is bright red, and I can't help but grin. I did it—I took down a bully.

It's then that the teacher finally turns up. "What's going on here?"

Daddy does get to walk me today. From the principal's office.

It's the day I learn that I can't tackle mean people. I need to use my words.

Daddy says, "Every situation has a different way to approach it. Just like football. Different plays end up with different results. You need to use your mind to work out the best move. You have to read the play, baby girl."

Then he adds, "Good job taking her down, but no more tackles at school."

T hree days passed, and everyone all but forgot what happened on that first day. My hands are almost healed, and my knees scabbed over.

"Let's play chase," Hunter suggests while we hang out on the playground.

Jace nods, and I giggle as I say, "I will give you the count of five...run."

Since I'm a fast runner, I always give them five seconds before starting to make it more of a challenge. I count down then jump up and run. Hunter is faster than Jace, but I want Jace to feel like the winner today, so I sprint as fast as I can after Hunter. He sees me coming, and with that glint in his eye, speeds up. He loves when I chase him.

I'm gaining on him, my chest burning and heart racing. I'm so close, I reach forward to grab him, my fingers still inches away.

Then, Hunter's whole body stops suddenly as he slams into the chest of a big boy who'd stepped out in front of him. Hunter crumples to the ground, the sad look in his eyes telling me everything I need to know. This boy did it on purpose. He is a bully just like the tall, mean girl.

"Fuck off," the boy says, and my mouth drops open. He said a bad word. Hunter tries to get up. The mean boy pushes him down again.

"Hey, get off him." I storm up to the mean boy.

He's a new boy, and I've seen him in my class but don't know his name. Yesterday, he pushed around kids on the playground and didn't talk to anyone in class. He's taller than me and has dirty blond hair and blue eyes. They would be pretty if they weren't on such a mean bully.

"Hey, what did you do to my friend?" Jace says beside me, out of breath.

The big boy shoves Jace's shoulder, causing him to fall down in the dirt next to Hunter.

"What the hell was that for?" I demand, my hands in fists as I put them on my hips like my mom does when she is telling me off. I want to punch him, but I remember what Daddy said. I have to read the play. No more fighting. Use my words.

Hunter stands and brushes his hands down his dirty tee. I'm reaching out to pluck a leaf from his shoulder when a hand comes out and pushes Hunter back down again.

My whole body is trembling. We're in a part of the school that doesn't have many students or teachers around. It's just the four of us, alone.

"Why did you do that again?" I ask, trying to calm down and not yell.

He shrugs.

Daddy said read the play...read the play.

The boy in front of me is skinny, tall, and he looks like he never brushes his long hair. That's why it looks dirty all over the place. It's long, down to his chin.

He puts his hands on his hips and glares at me. I narrow my eyes at him. Would he dare push a girl?

I rake my eyes over him again and see a bruise on his arm as *he shifts his stance. It isn't a normal looking one. It almost looks like the shape of a hand. I glance back at his face, and he pulls his arm closer to his body to hide the marks.*

Cocking my head to the side, I arch a brow at him. Did someone hurt him? Is that why he hurt Hunter and Jace? Was he hurting my friends because he's angry at someone?

A lot goes through my mind. Maybe he has a mean mommy like me. My mommy gets mad and hits me sometimes, and daddy gets angry at her. She's made my skin go red but hasn't left any bruises.

"Are you okay?" I whisper, low.

I didn't want Hunter and Jace to hear me. I don't think they would see the same things I did. The boy's face turns down in a frown, and he clenches his fists.

I don't even think, I move forward and wrap my arms around his torso. He stiffens at first, then tries to pry me off. I hold on tightly as Hunter asks in a strained voice, "What are you doing, Lala?" It's the nickname he uses for me when he is scared or worried. I don't want Hunter to be scared though.

I look up into the boy's eyes and smile. He freezes, his eyes now pinned on me.

"I'm giving him a hug, silly. Can't you see, Hunter?"

"But...but, why?" Jace asks from my left.

I don't look away from the boy, feeling him relax a little under my arms. He never takes his eyes from me as I nod. I want him to know it's okay. I'll take care of him. I won't let any mean people hurt him.

"Sometimes, people need a hug, and I like giving hugs."

"But...but he hurt me, Lala." Hunter sniffles.

"I know, but I think he's okay now. He just needed a hug, is all."

I slowly let go of the boy, and he stands there watching

Hunter and Jace behind me. When his eyes hit mine, I can see I made the right play.

"What's your name?" I ask.

"Roman," he grumbles, kicking dirt with his shoe. It has a hole in the top with his toe peeking out.

"Do you have any friends, Roman?" I ask him.

He blinks a few times before he shakes his head just a little.

"Oh, well, you're in luck. We've been looking for a new friend. Want to be ours?"

I hear Jace make a strangled sound as I smile at this sad boy who needs hugs and friends, nodding at him to say yes.

"No," he says as he storms away.

"Why would you want him to be our friend, Mila? He was mean, he hurt Hunter's arm."

I turn to Hunter and see he's holding his wrist.

"Because he needs one. And we are the three best friends ever. We are perfect friends for him." I hug Hunter and walk him to the nurse.

Every day that week, Roman sought us out. He would push Hunter down. Would shove Jace every chance he got and stood there as I hugged him.

The next week, he did the same, but this time I told him I wouldn't hug him anymore if he was mean to my friends. "I don't hug mean people, Roman. I only hug the nice ones."

For three days, Roman avoids us. I watch him out of the corner of my eye, hoping he will come over and be friends with us. He watches me too. No matter where I am, he's there. In the halls or after school at the gate. But I don't say anything to him. I know I can't. It's part of the play. He has to come to us.

On the fourth day, he walks up to me. Hunter and Jace freeze as Roman stands an inch from me and looks down into my eyes.

"Can I be your friend?" he mumbles.

My whole face smiles as I giggle. "You always were my friend, Roman. Can I be yours too?" I wrap my arms around him in a hug.

He hugs me back.

SIX
MILA

t's now midnight, and Dad text me to say he's so sorry, but he's still stuck there. I tell him it's okay because I'm heading to bed. But how can I when there's a party outside my window?

I peer out, trying to see if I can spot Grady. Going over to say hi would give me an excuse to be there, since Jace had decided to be an asshole and not invite me. But can I really blame him? I haven't seen Hunter or Roman anywhere.

I've looked them up on social media, but Roman doesn't have an account. Or, if he does, it's super private. Hunter and Jace do.

Hunter looks good, like *I wanna lick his abs* kind of good. He was always cute, but now he has filled out, and the grown-up version of his wicked grin is more than a little enticing. Girls likely throw themselves at him with very little effort on his part.

Jace looks hot too, but after the cold welcome he gave me earlier, he isn't as appealing. Hot assholes don't do it for me. If they did, Malcolm Junior would make my knees weak, even though he's my stepbrother. But, nope, he's just an asshole.

The music grows louder. It's as if they're taunting me. Fuck this. Fuck Jace.

Throwing my sheet off, I roll out of bed. My bare feet hit the carpet, and I jump up and down on the spot, punching the air a few times. "Fuck Jace."

I search my closet for something appropriate, since I don't have everything here. Mom said she would ship the rest to me. Yeah, right. She would rather burn my belongings than let me have them.

I pull out my short jean shorts—they hug my ass in all the right places—and a deep purple V-neck tee that clings to my curves. I might not have grown taller in four years, but my boobs sure got bigger. I'm proud of what I've been blessed with. They are more than enough.

Yanking my hair tie out, I let my hair fall around my face in waves. I shake it out and get to work on my face. Dark mascara and smoky eyeshadow make my cobalt-blue eyes pop. I also look a little badass. Mom hates it. That's probably why I love it so much. She's not here to complain about my make-up choices anymore.

I shove my phone in my back pocket and skip down the stairs and out the front door. The air is still warm and feels nice as I round the hedge between our properties and make my way down Jace's driveway.

"Holy shit. Mila? Mila Hart? No fucking way." A circle of guys opens up, and one emerges with his arms wide open.

"Emerson Henty." No way. Holy fuck. Something must be in the water here, because he was this skinny little kid who wore the thickest glasses I'd ever seen. Now he's all grown up and looks so different from how I would have imagined. Like, talk about a glow up. Dang.

He laughs and nods, pulling me into a hug. He spins me around a couple times before putting me back on my feet. He smells so good, I can't help but wonder what cologne he wears.

"Holy shit, when did you get back? Jace and the guys didn't say you were coming back. Are you, like, back for good?"

I laugh, shrug, and nod. "Yeah, I'm back for good. But Jace forgot my invite."

He doesn't question it. He wraps his arm around my shoulder and directs me over to his friends. "Hey, guys, this is Mila Hart. The most badass girl from my childhood. She kicked my ass in football practice every week when we were kids. She tackled my ass into the dirt so hard, I thought for sure I would break a bone."

"Didn't you play flag football?" one guy asks, and Emerson nods and chuckles.

He squeezes me tighter to him, the grin on his face contagious. I smile back, remembering that I'd done just that. It got me in trouble each week. He wasn't the only one I'd tackled. I'd tackled everyone. I might have had a problem back then.

"Yeah, but Mila didn't care. She went for the tackle, and if she hadn't, I don't think I would be as good as I am now. Forced me to learn how to keep my balance."

I laugh and put my hand on his chest, patting his very hard pec as I glance up at him. "Someone needed to kick your ass. I was honored to be the one to do it."

We talk for a bit, and I learn he's on the football team with Jace, Hunter, and Roman. That doesn't surprise me, but what does surprise me is that Jace is their quarterback.

That's news to me. I didn't internet stalk him enough before I came over here. But this is better, getting information from a close source.

"Oh, hey, they're inside if you want to go say hi."

I nod with a wicked grin. "Yeah, I should say hi. It would be rude not to."

He shakes his head and laughs. "Come on, girl, I got your back."

I let him lead me inside the house, the music softens once I close the door behind me. It's easier to talk in here.

I make my way through to the living room, stopping short when I catch sight of all three guys. Roman sits quietly, a beer in his hand as his eyes roam between Hunter and Jace. He looks the same, but older. Same dirty blond hair, except now I know that's the color and not because it's actually dirty.

Hunter has a dark-haired girl on his lap. She's giggling and touching his chest, and he pulls her close, kissing her. I feel a small stab of jealousy, even though it's illogical. I can't be jealous of my old friend hooking up. I'd known this would happen one day, but it should have been something I adapted to over time. Having it thrust into my face so quickly is jarring. But it's Jace that holds my attention.

Britney *fucking* Montlake.

She hangs off him, kissing his throat and staring at him like a lost puppy that just found its owner. And Jace is that owner. She throws her head back and laughs...until her eyes meet mine and she freezes. Jace notices the shift and sits up straighter in the armchair.

"Mila, what the fuck?" Jace growls out. I plaster on a fake smile as I move into the room. Gotta fake it to make it.

"Hey, guys. Long time, no see. Guess Jace forgot my invite."

Hunter moves the girl off his lap, and she squeaks. He starts to stand, but Jace makes a throaty sound, and Hunter's shoulders drop as he sits while watching me.

"Holy shit, Mila. You're really back." His eyes roam up my legs and settles on my mouth. His tongue dips out, and he wets his lower lip, nodding slowly to himself.

"I'm back. I don't know what Jace told you, but I'm here to stay."

Roman watches me out of the corner of his eye. The hand holding his beer is now fisted tightly. I'm a little worried he'll smash it and end up with glass embedded in his hand.

"Hell yeah, Mila," Hunter responds, looking genuinely happy to see me.

Roman doesn't speak. He just turns to Jace. Like, when did Jace become the one they turn to? What happened while I was gone?

"You need to leave, Mila. You weren't invited, and you never will be. We don't want you here," Jace says in an almost bored tone.

I watch as Britney practically humps him like a bitch marking her territory. She's not a lost puppy, like I first thought. She's a bitch in heat. "Yeah, you have to leave. Jace is my boyfriend."

My brows raise at that. "Really? You're dating Britney?" The words are out of my mouth before I can even think.

That's truly the biggest surprise so far. Jace—the boy who couldn't stand Britney to the point he would fake being sick just to get her to go away—is now dating her?

Jace doesn't answer. He just wraps his arm around Britney and pulls her closer. She beams over at me, like she won a prize and I lost. But I wasn't playing a game. She doesn't have to worry about losing her precious Jace. She can have him. If this is his reaction to my return, then they deserve each other.

"Don't act all surprised. I knew when we were picked as partners on the school field trips that Jace and I were meant to be." Britney puffs up her chest and looks down her nose at me as if waiting for me to challenge her.

I blink. Is she for real? "You were picked because he's a Montero, and you're a Montlake. It wasn't some magical matchmaking scheme by the teachers. It was alphabetical order."

God, what a dumbass.

"No, it wasn't," she huffs out, plastering herself against Jace.

I see his eye twitch…just a little. He doesn't like this, me being in his space. He wants me to leave, but at the same time, he wants me to witness this. To make me upset? Jealous? I have no idea what his goal is, but I love it even more because it isn't working, and that's annoying him.

"If that's the case, Britney—" I turn to the other guys. The girl is back on Hunter's lap, eyeing me, and Roman still won't face me. "Hunter and Roman should be madly in love right now and…"

Someone behind me laughs, and I spin to see Emerson moving farther into the room. He grins, knowing where this is going.

"I guess I'm supposed to marry Emerson here," I conclude.

Jace stands, and Britney almost topples off him, catching and righting herself at the last moment. He points to the door behind me. "Get the fuck out, Mila."

Britney sticks her chest out. "Yeah, you weren't invited.

And it's true that Jace and I are meant to be. He used to hold my hand. No one made him, but he did it. You just can't handle I'm with him, Mila. But you left, and he was fair game. Jace is mine. Forever."

I bite my lower lip to stop from laughing. The look on Jace's face at the word *forever* is priceless. Nevertheless, he growls at me, like I'm the one pledging my eternal love.

He made his bed. Not me. I throw my hands up. If we were gonna do this…then let's do this.

"Britney, Jace held your hand because you cried for your mom every field trip without fail, and you wouldn't walk, you would stand there and cry. He held it to keep you moving so the rest of us could enjoy ourselves. You made every school outing a nightmare with your sobbing, and Jace told everyone that you smelled and called you Stink-ney. If you were ever wondering where that nickname came from, you have been kissing that very mouth."

Britney screams and lunges for me, but Jace manages to grab her before she can get me. His face reddens as he glares daggers at me. Probably because he's guilty. He gave her the nickname in second grade, and he very well knows it. Everyone called her that up until I left.

She's spouting off a bunch of words my way as Jace tries to calm her down. Emerson moves in closer, his body pressing up against mine as he whispers into my ear, "Hey, Mila…you wanna go for a walk?"

I know what he means by that, but I'm not here to hook up with someone. That wasn't the plan.

I watch my old friends. Jace is calming Britney down, the girl on Hunter's lap is sucking on his neck as he watches me out of one eye, and Roman looks stiff and hasn't moved at all. His eyes now on me, I shiver from his intense gaze. He's changed the most out of the three of them. He looks older than his sixteen years.

"Nah, let's stay here and have some fun." I tell Em.

Jace looks over at me now. His face is unreadable.

Emerson sits down on the empty end of the sofa, and I observe Jace's expression as I move in to sit with Em. I watch the way his jaw ticks, and I know I'm pissing him off to the extreme.

Em pats the spot beside him, but I glance once more over to Jace before straddling Em. His large hands go to my waist as he pulls me in close, so I can feel what he's hiding under those jeans. Maybe a walk isn't such a bad idea. Nothing like a good fuck to relieve some tension.

With a smirk, I grind down on him. Em sucks in his lower lip and groans a little as he tilts his head back. "Fuck, Mila, did I tell you how sexy you are?"

"Em, she isn't staying, man." Hunter finally speaks up after being quiet through the whole Britney thing. I'd started to think he might want me here. But I guess the boss man said, "No Mila," so he was being a good boy and telling me to leave.

I peer at Hunter under my lashes and raise a brow before arching my back and pressing my chest against Em. My nipples peak and the friction sends little flutters lower. Hunter shifts a little, watching as I run my finger up Em's arm.

Jace growls my name again, and Hunter tries to hide his smile as I wink at him. He knows I'm pushing Jace's buttons. But in a new way that I had never done before. I don't know why I'm loving this so much, but I am.

Is Jace jealous? I hope so.

"Fuck you guys," Em declares. "I always had the hots for Mila. Now she is all grown up and rocking this hot ass body against mine. No way is she leaving...unless it's with me."

Jace grumbles something as he runs his hands through his hair. It looks messy and sexy. Ugh...no one can piss me off like him.

Why can't we go back to being friends? Why does he have to be an asshole? Yeah, okay, it's been four years, but he could at least understand that those years have been just as hard on me. Did he ever think that I lost all my friends and my father on the same day? No, he's only thinking about himself.

Roman, my big teddy bear. He'd loved to hug me. Every day I would wake knowing I was getting a Roman hug, and they were the best. No one saw him the way I did. Everyone was scared of him. Even now, I can tell not much has changed on that front. The only other girl in the room watches him warily. Like she wants to reach out and comfort him, but if she did, he would bite her head off.

"Fine, have her. No one else wants her," Jace calls over to Em.

Well, that hurts.

Em chuckles and I feel it reverberate through my chest. He wraps his arm around me as I sit up, trying to hold me close.

"Who said I wanted anyone else? I didn't. So, you don't need to worry. I'm not gonna be chasing after you, Hunter, or Roman."

Jace straightens and watches me as Em slides his hand up my back and into my hair. Em is huge...everywhere. His hand grips my hair a little, enough pressure to cause me to gasp and arch my back. Dang, Em was good at this.

"Yeah, Em, you can have her. Just know that I was her first kiss. I was there first."

It's like a bucket of cold water hits me while Hunter sits there, his eyes boring into mine, as the room slowly registers what he just said. *Fuck.*

"What the fuck?" Jace is back up on his feet. Britney thumps to the ground without a chance to right herself. I would have laughed if I didn't know where this is going.

Meanwhile, Hunter moves the girl off his lap to sit beside him. He's a little nicer with his toys than Jace is.

Roman also stands, his broad chest and the sharp lines of his jaw more prominent as he towers above the other two. He's so tall now. God, he's sexy too. Like a Viking. I shake my head to clear my thoughts. This isn't good. The room seems much smaller now, and I need to hide from the three of them.

Hunter holds his hands up as he faces Jace. "Look, man. I know, alright? I broke the pact. But I didn't think she was coming back, so when she came to me and asked me to be her first kiss, I couldn't say no. You wouldn't have either."

Jace is mad, but not at that. I know exactly what he's going to say next. Pushing away from Emerson, I quickly stand. I take a few steps back, but Jace pins me with his glare, his finger pointing at me. "You came to me on that last day and asked me to be your first kiss. So, which one was it, me or Hunter?"

Hunter spins to face me, then Jace. "What the fuck? You kissed her?" he yells. I hear the anger and confusion in his voice and grit my teeth as I watch the two of them square off with each other.

"You just said I wouldn't have said no. You were right —I didn't when she asked *me* to be her first."

"You weren't her first kiss. I was. It was right before her mom came to take her. She rode to my house on her bike and asked me to be her first kiss. She was leaving at two and came to me at…fuck." Hunter's brow furrows as he looks down at his fingers. Is he counting? Shit.

"She came to me that same day. Told me she didn't want to go away and wanted to have her first kiss with me. I was her first."

"What time did she come to you?" Hunter questions Jace.

"How should I know? It was four years ago. I didn't look at the time and mark it on my calendar. But it was before you. I would have known if I wasn't her first."

Jace is no longer watching me, so I start backing up. Em waves at me to leave, and I planned to do exactly that. That is, until Roman steps forward between them while they argue over the time of day.

They stop and watch as Roman approaches until he's towering over me. His impenetrable stare drills into me. It's as though all the air has left my lungs, and I'm choking on the weight of it. "Which one of us was your first?"

I swallow and inhale a ragged breath. Fuck him, fuck Hunter, fuck Jace…fuck them all.

Hunter and Jace stand there, speechless. And that's my cue to run. I spin on my heels and bolt out of there.

I'm the only one who knows the truth on who was my first.

But I will never kiss and tell.

SEVEN
HUNTER

When she walked into Jace's living room, I was a goner. My heart stopped for a moment, then started again, the same as it did for her all those years ago. Yeah, we made a pact. We were young and dumb. I didn't understand back then that if we made the pact that someone else would end up getting the girl.

It wasn't until she came to me and told me she wanted me—Hunter West—to be her first kiss that I realized the huge mistake we'd made. But it was too late. She was leaving.

I'm outside in my yard, throwing a stick for my dog, Chewy, to catch. Mom and Dad are inside arguing about something again, and I don't want to be here. But the boys are home today. No one wanted to do anything because she's leaving.

Mila, the girl who has been my best friend since I was six, is leaving, and I don't know if I will see her again. It isn't fair. I'd cried this morning, and I didn't even care if the others found out. She had been such a big part of my life up until now. I couldn't imagine life without her.

Chewy brings the stick back, and I reach for it with my bandaged hand. I feel the pull of the skin where it was cut, but I welcome the pain. It means she's still real to me. She exists.

She told me we'll be together again one day. But I want that day to be today and every day after. I don't want her to leave me. I need her more than she knows.

Glass shatters against a wall inside the house, then the slamming of doors. I sink my knees into the grass. Why do they always have to fight? Why can't they see me, see I'm upset? Why is it always about them, and I'm always an afterthought?

Chewy gives up when I don't throw the stick and runs off.

I hear the sound of my dad's car pulling out of the drive. He always leaves and goes to his office after a fight. Mom stays home, but she'll leave me for a bottle of whiskey in her room. I wouldn't see her until tomorrow.

Everyone leaves me.

"Hunter?"

I glance up, my eyes blurry from the tears. I wipe my face with the back of my hands and see an angel running toward me.

"Hunter? What are you doing?"

I scramble up, confused. Am I dreaming? She's supposed to be leaving today. Mila isn't really here. I'm dreaming and wishing she was, and now that's all I can see.

"Are you okay? You look like you saw a ghost." Mila chuckles, and I look around my yard. This is my yard…this is the girl I'm in love with, standing in front of me. She's really here.

"What are you doing here? Don't you have to leave today?"

She shrugs and giggles. Whenever she giggles, it gives me butterflies. The sound of her happiness always does that to me. She hasn't laughed for a few days, so the sound is like music to my ears. My own smile appears for the first time in days too.

"Yeah, I have to leave at two. But I couldn't leave without asking you something."

Her blonde hair is up in a high ponytail, and she reaches for it, pulling it in front of her. It's one of her signs, I know she's nervous right now. Mila doesn't do that very often; she's always so strong. I'd only seen her do it a handful of times, and one of those times was a few weeks ago.

We had gone to the lake; it was just a regular day. Not that any day could be considered regular when Mila was wearing a bikini. I'd had many, um, dreams about that bikini. It was embarrassing. Okay, it was all I could think about. My body responded to hers in a way I hadn't known it would, and last week, I'd almost drowned while trying to hide what was happening in my swim trunks.

She was sitting in the grass watching Jace and Roman swim. I walked up to her and sat beside her. "Why aren't you out there, swinging off the rope?"

I was chicken on that rope, something she teased me about. But I didn't hate the taunts, she wasn't being mean. It always made her giggle that I wouldn't do it.

"I don't feel good." Her brows were pinched, and she put her hand on her tummy.

"Oh no, are you going to be sick?"

She shook her head, then her eyes widened. She looked at her bike, then back to me. She went to stand but then sat back down just as fast.

"Do you think I could borrow your basketball shorts to ride home?" she asked, looking down at my black baggy shorts.

I wasn't going to swim today. I'd realized my basketball shorts were loose enough that if something were to happen, and I got another boner, she wouldn't notice it.

"What? No."

I had on my black boxers underneath, and those wouldn't

hide anything from her. They were tight. Why would she want my shorts? She wore her bikini on her bike all the time. She didn't even bring a towel, as she always said, "If we ride fast, it's like a dryer."

"Um..." She pulled her hair forward and started running her fingers through it. She didn't look at me, instead watching as Roman dunked Jace under the water. I sat there quietly for a few moments not knowing what to do. "I think...no, I know. I just got my period."

Her big blue eyes were watering like she was about to burst into tears.

"That thing we learned about in sex ed?"

I was panicking now. I didn't want to freak her out, but was she going to be okay? I didn't listen well to the girl part; I was still freaked out about the boy part. Like how everyone else in class had known that's how babies were made, and I hadn't. My parents never told me that stuff. Even Mila and the boys knew, and I sat there and tried to pretend I did. It finally made sense to me why I was washing my sheets almost every morning.

But the period...that was the blood part. She was bleeding? I looked to the water, to the tree, back to Mila. I didn't know what to do. Should I call her dad?

"Yes, and I don't want anyone to see when I ride home." She sniffled.

"Hey, what are you doing, Mila? Come in, we can race," Jace called out, waving his arm, and I saw her stiffen. This was bad.

"Should I get my mom?" I could ride really fast home and get her. I was sure she hadn't been drinking today, so she could come and get Mila. Take her to the hospital? Home?

But Mila shook her head. "No, if you give me your shorts, I can go home. I promise I will wash them, Hunter. I just...I didn't." She buried her head in her arms, and I felt a pang in my chest. She was embarrassed, and I didn't want her to be. I knew all the sex stuff was kinda icky and weird, but I didn't want her to be sad.

"You can have my shorts." I moved to pull them off and kicked at them when they got stuck to my shoes. I handed them to her, and she whispered, "Thanks."

Jace called out again, only he was closer now, and I heard her suck in a gasp. "Hey, we will be there in a minute." I moved forward to block Mila from the boys. When she got my shorts on, she stood. I turned just as she pulled the drawstring tight.

"Thanks, Hunter."

Mila left and didn't come back to swim for three whole days. The boys complained about how she was slacking off this summer. But when I told my mom what had happened, she told me that I did the right thing. Mila just needed a few days because periods could make you feel sick and crabby.

But now, when she's supposed to be getting on a plane, she's in my yard…nervous. Is it because she got her period again and needs my shorts?

I decide not to wait for her to tell me. I tug my shorts down and hold them out to her. She looks from me to the shorts and then back to me before bursting into giggles.

"No, I don't need your shorts today, Hunter."

Now I feel silly and quickly pull them back on. I want to hug her and tell her she can stay with me. I will hide her in my house so her mom can't find her, and I will feed her pizza and strawberries. Her favorites.

"Why are you here?"

She looks down at her feet then glances at me under her lashes. A small smile is there as she licks her pink lips. "I want you to be my first kiss, Hunter."

I take a step back, stunned. Did she really ask me that? She *wants me to be her first kiss? Not Jace. Not Roman. Me. Unable to form words, I point to my chest, and she nods.*

I open my mouth to say yes, but all I can do is stutter. I nod and she smiles.

She moves in close, her hands going to my shoulders, and I place mine on her hips. For a brief moment, I think about the pact I have with the boys. But that leaves my mind just as fast as it entered. She wasn't coming back. They wouldn't know, and I wanted to be her first kiss. I wanted her to be mine.

The butterflies in my belly start dancing, and I draw closer, my lips puckered. I close my eyes as her warm lips brush against mine.

It's like fireworks and cherry snow cones and jumping into the lake on a hot summer day. Kissing Mila is all of my favorite things wrapped up into one perfect moment. I love her and want to marry her and, even though it's kinda icky, have babies with her. She's the girl for me.

"The fuck?" Roman yells, jolting me out of my memories and back to the party. His fist is balled in Emerson's tee, who holds his hands out in surrender.

"Fuck, I was just asking. Because of the pact you were talking about, it sounds like Mila's fair game, and I can ask her out."

"No," all three of us yell at the same time.

Emerson's eyes widen right before Roman throws him back against the couch. A girl screams as he lands beside her. I look over and notice it's the girl who was all over me earlier. She peers up at me with those fake lashes, and I shake my head. I don't want her anymore. Not after seeing Mila.

Mila was going to be the end of me. I still want her, after all this time. But now I'm also pissed. I need to know who was first. It makes sense that she would have kissed Jace last when she rode her bike home. But my house is the same distance away from her place as Roman's but in opposite directions. She would've had to ride past her area of town before going to the other. She came to me around lunch time. Would that have even been enough time to get to Roman's, then get home and kiss Jace, then leave?

"I was first," Jace growls at us as Britney comes up beside him, placing her hand on his arm. He spins on her, and her eyes widen.

"What does it matter, baby? I will be your last."

And that was the wrong thing to say, obviously. Jace loses it. He shrugs her off and screams at everyone to leave. The party is over. When she tries to grab him again, he yells, "Leave, now."

Nothing shuts a party down faster than finding out the girl you've loved your whole life lied to you about your first kiss.

The music stops, and the sounds of cars and people leaving echo around us. The three of us don't speak until things are quiet outside.

Jace turns to me, then faces Roman. His jaw ticks as he takes a deep breath. "This is why we have the pact. Did you see what's happened already? She played us all. She left for four years without a word, and in just a few minutes with her back in our lives, she had us all at each other's throats."

Roman grumbles in agreement, and as much as I want to tell them both to fuck the pact, I know it's the truth. It was just as Jace had said when we were ten. She would pick one, breaking us apart. Look at tonight, all that over a kiss. One little kiss, and we were fighting. Imagine how it would be if she did pick one of us.

These guys have been my best friends for so long. They're my brothers, and I would do anything for them. Even tamp down and hide the feelings I still have for Mila. I won't let her come between us. I need them as much as they need me.

All three of us place our right hands over each other's and call out loudly like we had many times as kids.

"The pact still stands."

EIGHT
MILA

'd expected Jace to storm over, demanding to know who my first kiss was, after I heard everyone at the party leave shortly after me. But nothing.

Sunday was uneventful too. I didn't see Jace or the guys at all. Dad took me out for school supplies, and we picked up pizza and ice cream for dinner. It was a great day. I loved being back with Dad.

Monday morning came too fast, and now I have to face them. I'm beginning to rethink my choice of school. It wouldn't be a problem if the truth about that kiss—those kisses—hadn't risen to the surface so fast. I had found out they had this pact together weeks before I left. I had over-heard them talking about it when they thought I was in the bathroom. I was upset at first, I thought they had left me out because I was a girl. But then I understood it enough to understand that even if they *like* liked me, they wouldn't act on their feelings. That's why I wasn't part of their pact.

I didn't think something like my first kiss would blow up in my face so quickly. I knew it would come up...eventually. It wasn't like I forgot about it. I remembered that day very well. I had just hoped we were all friends again when it came out and I could approach them about it before it got to what it did on Saturday.

After dropping by the office to pick up my schedule, I'm off to class. The map the secretary gave me isn't the best. I couldn't understand where my locker was when she pointed it out, so she offered to ask a student to give me a tour. But I didn't want that either. Instead, I stuff my phone in my back pocket and wander the busy halls until I find my first class—English with Mrs. Becker.

I'm the last one to class, and when I walk in, all eyes are on me. But my gaze focuses on two students in this class. "You have to be kidding me," I mutter under my breath. How many students go here? And how the heck did I end up with double trouble in my first class of the day?

"Find a seat, there are two spares." Mrs. Becker waves to a seat beside Roman, and the other is beside a girl with red hair.

Roman and Jace glare at me.

It's a difficult choice. If I pick the girl, the safe spot, will Roman think I'm scared of him. That I'm not willing to fight for his friendship? But if I sit next to Roman, how much worse will my day get?

When Roman slams his backpack down on the desk beside him, I get the message loud and clear. I'm not welcome there. There's no place for me in our group. Their group.

I sit beside the girl and open my bag, grabbing my books.

"Hi, Mila, I'm Eva. Do you remember me?"

I face the girl and immediately recognize her. "Oh,

wow, Eva. I remember you." She used to have frizzy red hair, and her mother braided it every day when we were in elementary school. I used to look at her hair with envy. I wished my dad could braid like that. It's straight now and hangs over her shoulder, still the most beautiful color.

"I heard you were back and that there was a fight at Jace's party over you."

Wow, I expected something to be mentioned, but I'm not even five minutes into class and it's happening.

"That's not what happened. Were you there?"

I didn't see her there, but then I was kinda focused on three boys. She shakes her head and pulls out her phone, scrolling until she finds a dark, grainy video. It's of me standing there with Jace, Hunter and Roman looking down at me. You can't hear too much until Roman's deep voice demands, "Which one of us was your first?"

I snatch her phone and look at who had posted it. Summer Waters. Yeah, stupid name. Her parents were probably hoping for her to be a news anchor with that name, but it was more of a porn star name.

Mila Hart is breaking hearts again. We always wanted to know which one she was fucking. Guess we don't have to wonder anymore. She was fucking them all. She lied to them. They all thought they were her first. #whore

My blood boils. This is why I hate social media. It's like no one is concerned about the truth anymore. People twist the facts to suit their own purposes, not caring who's hurt in the process. I'm not hurt, let them think what they want about me. Water off a duck's back, I have thick skin. Hell, I needed it. I lived with my mom for four years. But others, they don't need this shit. Online bullying is out of hand.

I still have social media accounts, of course. But, at my old school, I did my best to keep my name out of any scandals. I wanted no part of the gossip and bullying. Still don't.

When I pass Eva's phone back to her, she's watching me with a gleam in her eye. "So, is it true? Did you have sex with them all and tell each one you were a virgin?"

Is she serious? It's like she wants it to be true.

"What the fuck? No. That's not it at all." Heat rises to my cheeks. Not from embarrassment. From anger. "For god's sake, I was only twelve when I last saw them. I wasn't having sex with them."

In spite of myself, I turn to find Roman with his arms crossed over his chest. It's when I first notice his tattoos. Holy fuck. They're amazing. So colorful, and even from here, I can tell the artwork was well done. A professional artist had done those, not some random guy with a tattoo gun.

Jace rocks back in his chair, watching me. As soon as my eyes meet his, he stops and crosses his arms. A devilish grin spreads across his gorgeous face. Clearly, he knows about the video and comment. Summer Waters was Britney Montlake's best friend the last time I was here. I have a feeling they're still besties.

When class ends, I can't help but notice the stares and whispers. My fellow students are pointing and staring at me. Everyone knows. Fan-fucking-tastic.

"Move." Jace shoves me to the side with his body as he exits the room. I step aside to let the rest of the students out and reach into my bag for the map. Chemistry.

I'm a few steps from the classroom when I stop in my tracks. This has to be a joke. I look down at my schedule and up again to see the three of them standing outside the classroom. Maybe they're just talking and they aren't in my class. Yeah right, why else would they be here?

But as I draw closer, they turn as one and stare at me. They're waiting for me. Do they have my class schedule? How else would they know I'm in this class?

With them watching me, I'm suddenly hyper-focused on how I look approaching them. I'm wearing denim shorts and a baggy white tee. Nothing special, but at least my legs look good in these shorts. But am I walking funnier than I normally do?

Ugh. Why do I even care?

Probably because they all stand there like Greek gods. They're each attractive in different ways, and I'm not the only one who notices. Other students check them out as they pass, and a few girls wave and giggle when Hunter winks at them.

Britney appears out of nowhere, Summer following her. Bitch. No way I'm gonna let that shit she said slide. I hate assholes, but I hate bullies more. And from what I have gathered. She is the mean girl and I won't stand for that shit.

"Hey, Summer. I saw the video and comment. Take that shit down. You know it's not true." I cock my head to the side and purse my lips as her eyes widen at the sight of me. Like she didn't expect to see me, or maybe didn't expect me to speak up about it. She knew me before. I never tolerated bullies previously, I wasn't about to change now.

But she straightens up, and her expression changes fast as she giggles. "No way. I have it straight from the source. It's true. That right, boys?"

Jace leans back against the wall, and Britney plasters herself to him, her leg wrapping around his. That's right, Britney. You better mark your property or someone will steal him. Won't be me, though.

"It's true," Jace replies casually.

I grit my teeth. Does he think this is going to…what? Hurt me? Make me go cry and disappear? I live next door to him, I know his parents, his brother. Hell, there would always be rumors about me and the boys. I'd lived with them already. But now that we were older, of course the rumors would be more sexual in nature.

I'm not even upset for myself. I'm upset for him. He wants to go to college and play football. That had always been his dream. Having this online wouldn't look good for college recruiters.

"Jace, you're just angry because you don't know who my first kiss is. I get it, but I was twelve, dumbass. You might want to be careful what you let spread around, because I'm pretty sure it's illegal to be having sex at that age."

I watch as his expression changes from one of smugness to realization that he fucked up. Yeah, boys are so dumb. I point at his school athletics T-shirt that says "Rebels of Ridgecrest High."

"Yeah, don't think your coach would like to know about you having sex with minors either. Might not get to play this season. But since you say it's true and all, I guess it is. Maybe I should let him know it came straight from the source."

Hunter straightens up, shaking his head, his hands up in defense. "Hey, wait up, Mila. It was a kiss. That's it. I'm telling you now, I had nothing to do with that." Hunter points at Summer. "Take that shit down now. I can't have that on my record."

He tries to take Summer's phone out of her hand while Jace whispers in Britney's ear, his eyes on me. Roman just stands there, not moving, though his eyes track me as I walk into the classroom.

"Emerson." I smile, my chest feeling lighter at the sight of him. He's sitting next to a guy I don't know.

"Mila, hey, you're here." Standing, he looks around and then down at the guy who's clearly on the football team.

"Hey, Leo, can you sit somewhere else so Mila can sit with me?"

I put my hand out. "No, you don't have to do that." I don't want him to move just because I'm here.

But Emerson isn't having it. "I think it's best you sit here. All of them are in this class, and they're not happy with you."

I laugh, because I'm more than aware of that fact.

Leo gets up. "Hey, I'm Leo. I was there on Saturday night, so I have no problem moving." He grabs his books, and I thank him as he moves a few seats back.

I don't waste any time sitting beside Em. "Fuck, Saturday night was crazy. I can't wait for the next party." Laughing, I bump my shoulder against his.

He chuckles and then freezes. Following his gaze, I see Jace and Britney stroll in, Roman and Hunter following. Hunter's on his phone and talking to Roman, showing him something. Maybe looking for posts about me from Saturday night. I have no doubt if Hunter's parents see that shit online, they'll be pissed. They'd always been set on him getting into Harvard. Which does shock me they let him go here and not Lakeview Prep.

The teacher finally stands up and tells the class to quiet down. "For those of you who haven't been in my class before, I assign seats based on a random draw. I have all your names in here. I will draw out two names, and that will be your partner. You will sit together and do all class assignments together. I won't change, and if you ask, I'll deduct a grade from your assignment each time."

I realize then that he doesn't have my name in there. As I walked in, I forgot to give him the slip from the office. Maybe this will spare me a partner. But when I quickly scan the room, I count an even number. Fuck. I hope whoever is last, isn't one of *them*.

Mr. Rayne starts rattling off names. Hunter is partnered with a girl with braces and a hot pink hoodie. I wonder how she can wear that thing. The cooling isn't the best in here, and I would melt in those clothes.

"Jace Montero and Emerson Henty."

"Fuck," Em whispers under his breath. I'm surprised. Based on their interactions Saturday night, I'd assumed they're friends.

"You come here," Jace calls out to him, and Em gets up and mouths, "Sorry." I shake my head. It's not his fault.

As everyone's name is called out but four, I keep my fingers crossed I'll be paired with Leo or the other girl I spot in the corner. Because the only other name who hasn't been picked is Roman's.

"Leo Anderson and Jessa Henderson."

Oh, fuck. I look over my shoulder to where Roman stands, waiting his turn. He knows what this means too.

"I only have one left—Roman Valentine. Who haven't I called out?" Mr. Rayne asks.

I raise my hand and duck my head, peering up at him.

"Sorry, and you are? I don't seem to have you on my class list."

"Mila Hart."

He adds my name to his class list and gestures for Roman to sit next to me.

The chair scrapes loudly as he sits down beside me. His

presence alone has me holding my breath, and I don't know why. He'd never hurt me, I know that much. At least I hadn't been paired with Jace. I would take Roman over him any day.

I can't resist studying his tattoos up close. I'm surprised there's so much color. I'd always imagined, if he was to get any tattoos, they would be dark. Not so vibrant.

They're amazing. I follow the full sleeve with my eyes, taking in the under the sea theme. There's a shark, a turtle, a fish, and a sunken ship. A tentacle wraps around his wrist, and I find myself reaching out to grab his arm. I want to see where it leads.

A deep grumble seeps from his chest, warning me, and I snatch my hand back. "Sorry. They're so beautiful, I got lost in admiring the artwork."

I don't expect him to respond, and he doesn't so much in words. But I watch as he slowly flips his palm over, exposing the octopus holding onto a treasure chest along his wrist and forearm. I'd known all wasn't lost with Roman.

He doesn't hate me. Not completely.

NINE
ROMAN

Mila Hart.

I'd imagined seeing her again, but at the same time, I'd hoped she was nothing but a memory.

When Jace said she was back, I didn't want to believe it. Memories of good times came flooding back, and I didn't want to think about that shit. It only made me weak, reminding me of everything I've lost in the past four years.

I'm angry she disappeared from my life. The last four years have been hell. I needed her, and she left me. She left me to deal with my drunk, junkie dad, the asshole who treats me like a worthless piece of shit. Without her here to chase the demons away, I've become more messed up than ever. Fighting away my pain and scars.

She'd always been in my corner, no matter what. I loved Mila Hart, and she tore my heart into shreds when she left.

Saturday night, she blew everything up. She destroyed me.

She was my first kiss. I was hers.

Or so I'd thought.

How could she lie to me like that? Our kiss had been my best memory. I'd held tight to the knowledge that she'd chosen me to be her first. That she'd wanted me, the boy who had nothing else to give her. I came from nothing; I could barely feed or clothe myself. All I could offer her was a hug every day. Even then, I'd been selfish. The hugs weren't for her…they were for me.

We'd picked daisies, and I would put the best one behind her ear. I didn't have anything else I could offer her but my love and protection.

That's over now.

All those memories have been tarnished with her lies.

I want to know the truth, want to know which one of us was first. Deep down, I know it wasn't me. Why would she pick me first when Jace lived right next door? They were friends since birth. And Hunter was charming, always making her laugh. But me…I was called quiet and moody by a few. Scary by most. And a worthless piece of shit by one.

I hadn't made her laugh with jokes. I hadn't known her forever. Why would she even come to me, unless it was out of pity? She'd kissed me so I wouldn't be left out. If Jace, Hunter and I had talked about it, we would have come to the conclusion she didn't want me to be the only one she didn't kiss.

But we never did. I hadn't wanted them to know I broke the pact, so I stayed away from them after she left. I was worried they would see it on my face. They would know I kissed her, and they wouldn't want to be friends with me anymore. They would leave me just like she did.

When they didn't question me about it, I knew they didn't suspect a thing. I held that secret from them. It wasn't the only secret I'd kept over the years. But I knew one day they would find out the truth. One way or the other, the truth always came out.

And it was always ugly.

Now I'm her partner in class like some cruel twist of fate. Of course my name was drawn last. I'm not someone who gets picked first for anything.

I don't know how to feel. I want her back in my life, but she doesn't know how dark and fucked up it has become. There are things I shield Hunter and Jace from. If I open up to Mila, I won't be able to hide those things from her. She'll see right through me. She could always see through my mask.

She smells nice. It was the first thing I noticed when I sat down beside her. She has changed so much, but so have I. She was just a few inches shorter than me before she left, now I tower over her with my six-foot three frame. Her hair is the same, always so shiny and smooth. My fingers itch to stroke it.

I hold myself stiff, willing myself to not look at her.

When she reaches out to me, my skin crawls, and I see red. I want to grab her wrist to stop her. I have to curl my fingers into fists to stop myself.

No one touches me. *No one.*

I grumble in warning. I can't form words in this state, and I don't want to hurt her. I want her to stay away.

No, that's not the truth. I don't want her to stay away; I need her to. It's best for both of us. With all the shit I'm mixed up in, I can't care about anyone. They will see it as a weakness to take me down.

"Sorry. They're so beautiful, I got lost in admiring the artwork."

Her voice hasn't changed. There's still a musical quality to it that makes my heart race. Like the first time we met, and she hugged me after I shoved Hunter and Jace down. She wasn't a normal girl, that's for sure. That's why we'd needed to form the pact. Why it has to stay in place. To protect ourselves from being hurt by the only girl who could ever break us apart.

I finally register what she'd said—she was talking about my tattoos. She wants to see more of them. I know what she's looking for, and if I show her this, she'll know how much she meant to me. Even now, do I want her to see that?

I do.

I flip my left hand over, exposing what completes the design. I had Ronnie down at the shop do this one. All summer, we worked on this tattoo. It might look like an underwater ocean scene, but it holds much deeper meaning.

No one would understand the importance of it unless they know me. There are three who know me. Two people who see what I let them. One person who knew the real me, but that was four years ago. A lot has changed in that time, and now I want her to see.

Will she know…?

I hear her intake of breath and glance at her out of the corner of my eye. Her hand is over her mouth, and she moves closer to me, her finger tracing the air close to my wrist but not touching. I hold still for a moment. She sees. She knows.

Realization strikes. I'm not ready for that box of

emotions to open. So, I yank my hand away and cross my arms over my chest to block her from seeing any more.

She hadn't forgotten me. She remembers, but that was the old me. Mila wouldn't like who I am now.

I don't even like me.

TEN
MILA

oly shit.

A football, a tutu, a sword, and a tiara.

That's what is in the treasure chest on Roman's arm.

My breath catches as tears spring to my eyes. It takes everything in me to hold them back. I want to hug him so badly, but he moved his arm away so I can't see it anymore. He knows that I realize what the tattoo means.

It's me. The chest is full of my treasure—the things the two of us played with as children.

I take a few deep breaths and try to listen to the teacher, but I can't focus on anything else. Roman hasn't forgotten about me. He all but wrote my name on his body. But much deeper than words ever would be.

I want to know more. I want to ask him what this all means. Why did he put that there? Does he miss me like I miss him? Will he talk to me now, or does he hate me like Jace?

My head swims with questions. Is Jace the shark, Hunter the turtle, and Roman the octopus protecting me?

Not that I'll be getting answers any time soon. It's obvious Roman is closed off now. He isn't going to give me anything more. He'd already given me more than I could have asked for when he showed me the rest of his tattoo.

The bell rings, and he leaves the classroom first. Not surprisingly, he can't get away from me fast enough.

Emerson walks out with me. "Hey, let's meet up at lunch. I'll save you a seat."

I nod and smile, but it doesn't reach my eyes. I'm still wrapped up in that treasure chest and all my treasure in it.

Em's offer is a relief, though. At least I have one friend here. Might not be the three I'd originally expected, but one is better than none.

Lunch rolls around, and the cafeteria is busy by the time I arrive. I line up behind some girls and listen as they discuss Jace and how hot they think he is. How Britney needs to move aside and let the rest of them have a turn.

When one of them says she's going to lure Jace away from Britney, convinced he'll fall in love with her once he gets to know her, I scoff.

She turns to me. "Excuse me, but don't you know it's rude to listen to other people's conversations?"

I chuckle. Is she serious? She'd practically broadcast her plans to lure Jace away to the entire school. I'm surprised Britney isn't over here, clawing her eyes out.

"When the conversation is that loud, I can't not hear it. But good luck with it all."

They all turn to face me now, eyes narrowed, and the

sneer on lure girl's face is priceless. Making friends everywhere today, it seems. "Oh my god, you're the new girl. The one who fucked all three of them. When you said they were each your first, I guess one in each hole would make sense."

Okay, I need to accept that this is going to be the day that everyone talks shit about me. Probably more like a week, since Jace obviously has a fan club. At least I know the drill. It will all be forgotten when something else happens to give them something else to buzz about.

"I'll tell you a little secret about Jace." All four of them come closer, like the gossip-eating bitches I knew they were. "It was Jace. He was my first, but don't tell him."

All their faces form into an 'O' as they process the news. "No way, for real?"

I nod, even though it's a lie. Let him think he was first, if only for a day.

When I see Emerson sitting with the other football players, I decide I'm good to eat my slice of pizza and soda somewhere else. I dump my tray down on a table full of students. A couple inch away, not wanting to be caught associating with me.

Fair enough. I can respect not wanting to be on the other end of Jace.

It doesn't take long for the gossip to spread, and within five minutes, I hear Britney scream, "No, it's not true," while Jace looks over at me. Dang, those girls work fast. I need to remember their faces to avoid them.

It was a harmless lie.

Except, I realize my mistake the moment I see Roman. Then Hunter.

A harmless lie that hurts two others isn't harmless. I've turned into a bully. It's not a good feeling either. I messed up. I shouldn't have done that. I was just upset with Jace from earlier, and I lashed out.

I was just as bad as those girls, spreading rumors and lies to hurt others. This isn't like me, and guilt is already churning in my stomach.

Roman isn't looking at me—he's looking out the window—and Hunter's face falls, his eyes finding mine across the cafeteria. *Fuck.* If anything, I just made this so much worse. I upset and hurt two people I've never wanted to hurt.

Jace stands up and points at me. I shake my head and shrug. The expression changes as he narrows his eyes at me. Roman is glowering at me now and says something to Jace. Then all three of them watch me intensely, and my body thrums with nervous energy. I don't know what's about to happen, but Jace tilts his head as if to say "game on," and I know I shouldn't have played with fire.

D ad picks me up after school. He won't be able to do it again. This is only because it's my first day. I'd told him I can take the bus. I don't mind.

"I spoke with Ella today. It makes no sense, you catching the bus when the boys come here every day. They can give you a lift in the morning."

He called Jace's mom? I was about to protest when I realized I hadn't seen Grady yet. The school's big, and he's a senior this year, but I'd been hoping to see him. Even if he still thinks of me as an annoying little sister, I'm okay with getting a lift from him.

"Yeah, I'll go speak to Grady. Jace isn't really talking to me right now, Dad."

I feel, rather than see, him look over at me.

"Jace isn't talking to you? You used to be best friends. It wasn't your fault you had to move so far away. I knew you didn't like talking about them, so I didn't mention them when I called. But I didn't realize he wasn't speaking to you at all."

I shrugged. "It was my fault. I didn't talk to him while I was gone, even though he tried. It was just too hard." I take a deep breath; I'm beginning to understand how much I hurt them by not calling or telling them why. "I ignored all their calls and messages."

"Oh, Mila, baby. You should have told me. I could have helped. Now, you're here without friends."

"Don't worry, Dad. I have friends. My old friends are here, and it's been great seeing them today."

I don't want him to find an excuse to send me to Lakeview Prep. And I don't want him worrying about me being alone or something. I would work out the thing with the boys...hopefully.

"Well, I guess it would be best to speak to Grady. But, tonight, we have some special guests. If you remember."

"I finally meet Kate, Madison and…" I trail off, hoping Dad will fill me in on his name, because for the life of me I can't remember it.

"Asher."

Right, Asher.

Well, this better be good after the long ass day I'd had already.

⬤▸ ⬤▸ ⬤▸

Kate is beautiful, and Madison is the spitting image of her. They have this dark brown hair that's shiny and straight. Just so shiny…I need to ask them what they use, because mine is never that shiny.

They're both tall. It's like everyone is taller than me these days.

Asher…fuck. He is hot, and that's so bad to think about, because my dad really likes his mom. So much that I have a feeling one day Asher will be my stepbrother. So, I'm hoping he's an asshole. He's a football player, so chances are kinda high he is. Plus, that will help with any attraction there.

"Hey, it's nice to finally meet you. Coach talks about you all the time." Asher holds his hand out for me to shake. Okay, maybe he's just trying to be nice in front of my dad so he doesn't get kicked off the team.

I glance at my dad to find him beaming. Turning back to Asher, I say, "It's great to meet you too."

Is this handshake lingering a little longer than usual? Shit. Has dad noticed? Or am I just reading into this because Asher is gorgeous and that hair, like his mom's, is dark brown and styled just right.

Madison is wary of me and won't make eye contact, but Kate comes right in with a huge hug and smile. "Oh, Mila, I have heard so much about you. I think we will get along well." She then whispers in my ear, "Madison is a little shy, so she takes a while to come out of her shell. She isn't being rude like so many people seem to think."

I pull back and nod. I understand what she means. How someone being standoffish can be mistaken for snobbery. I'll have to make sure Madison feels comfortable around me, and hopefully we can be friends.

Kate hugs my dad and kisses him, laughing at him for burning the pasta he attempted for dinner. The way he lights up and laughs so freely with her, I know Kate's perfect for him. I'd never seen my dad like this with my mom. Not once.

And, yes, my dad, the chef. He didn't put enough water in the pot and left it on the stove for too long. He'd been busy watching game tapes and was only alerted to it when I yelled out from upstairs that there was a burning smell.

The smell is embedded into the house now. I tried to spray some perfume to cover it, but nothing did. So, we had the windows open even though it's warm out.

Dad decides that even pasta is too hard for him and orders takeout. I tell him he should have done that first. I can't cook either, so we were gonna have a lot of takeout in our future. I need to learn, since I can't live off pizza forever. Although it's a nice idea.

Madison is sitting on the sofa, so I sit beside her. "So… Madison. How was your first day of school?"

How was school? I sound like a parent.

She shrugs and gives me a tight smile.

"I had one of those days too. My old friends were being dicks, and some shit that went down over the weekend went viral, I guess. I wish it was something good, but nope, just another thing that was shit. But…they had pizza, so my day wasn't all bad. And now I get to meet you."

I can't believe I just said all that out loud. I was trying to make her feel more comfortable, but I kinda just spewed all my problems onto her.

"My friend Bella didn't talk to me all day. She sat at Everly Walker's table," Madison whispers as she plays with the hem of her sundress.

"Who is Everly Walker?" I ask, hoping she'll continue while the other three chat about the upcoming football season.

"She's the most popular girl, and now Bella doesn't want to be seen with me. I don't know why she would want to sit there. Those girls are mean. They always picked on us in middle school, and now she's one of them."

Oh, shit.

"For real? Bella sounds like she's a bitch to just ditch you like that. That's not a true friend if she chooses popularity over you."

"Are you serious, Mads? Bella ditched you?" Asher says from where he now stands next to us, sounding furious.

Madison nods, and the way her big brown eyes look up at her brother warms my heart. She's a girl who trusts her brother has always got her back.

"You should have come told me. You can sit with us for lunch. I'll see if I can get my schedule changed so you can."

That's the best idea. "I bet Asher sits with all the footballers too. She'll be jealous that you know them. The mean girls will want to come sit with you and be friends with you. And you can just tell them to leave."

Asher shakes his head. "I meant so she wasn't alone, Mila. But yeah, the team all sits together." He sticks his hands in his front pockets. "I knew she was up to something. Bella tried to ask me out over summer. I didn't want to tell you, and I had no interest in her in that way. I hope she isn't being like this because I told her no."

Madison shook her head. "I told her you would say no. You never date anyone."

Asher laughs. "'Cause who would want to deal with dating me? Football is my life right now. I don't have time for a girlfriend." Asher sits back on the sofa beside me and stretches his long legs out in front...they're so muscular. Shit, look away.

"Now I wish I was going to your school. I would sit with you. I have no friends to sit with at lunch either." Then I laugh, remembering the students I was sitting with inching away. "I'm the school's pariah, and I wish I was making it up, but I'm not. I'm sure you'll make new friends by the end of the week."

A fter dinner, Dad asks if we want dessert. Madison wants chocolate ice cream, and I want cookies and cream. We agree that we should go out and get some, but before we can leave, Madison gets a call from Bella. I think Bella might be apologizing, so Madison is in my bedroom so they can talk in private.

Dad and Kate are snuggling on the couch and watching an old football game, of all things. My dad and football, such a romantic. It makes me smile. This was my life growing up... Everything was football.

"Can you two go get the ice cream?" Dad asks.

Asher grabs his mom's keys. "Sure, want anything?"

They both shake their heads and start kissing and whispering. I'm a little grossed out by that. It's something I'll need to get used to but...like, get a room.

Asher grabs my arm and gestures with his head to the

front door. "Come on, let's get out of here before we have to see any more of that."

I snort. "How much have you had to put up with?"

"You don't wanna know. Like, let's just say…I have seen your dad in just his underwear. I had to bleach my eyes."

I burst out laughing, and he shakes his head and covers his eyes. But he has a huge smile.

"I had once seen Malcolm, my stepfather, naked when I was getting a late-night snack. I had to burn my eyes out after that one." I shiver at the memory. "So gross and wrinkly."

It's now Asher's turn to chuckle. "Okay, you had it worse."

On the way to the ice cream parlor, I learn more about Asher. He's a junior like me, he's sixteen, seventeen in October, and he plays for the Kings of Lakeview Prep as a wide receiver.

He doesn't plan to go far with it, just loves the game and loves to play. So, when he goes to college, it won't be for football. He wants to focus on his studies and get into robotics, which sounds techy and cool.

We grab the ice cream and go back home. As I get out of the car, holding ice cream for Madison and me, Asher rounds it to help me. "I got to say something."

I raise my brows and tilt my head as I peer up at him. He moves closer to me and pushes the car door closed. We're now standing only inches apart.

"I was kind of expecting you to be a bitch," he says seriously, and I burst out laughing. After a few seconds, his deep chuckle joins in.

"Why would you think that?" I bat my lashes at him with a cheeky smile.

He shrugs and chuckles deep again, taking the ice cream from me. "I just thought people from New York were all assholes, so I expected you to be one. Plus, you're like so…um, I don't think I should say, but you're pretty."

I can't shake the smile from my face. This is just so funny. "You think I'm pretty?" I twirl on the spot and curtsey.

He shakes his head trying to hide his smile and looks up to the night sky, letting out a deep breath. "You know you are, so don't push me for more. Because when I saw you, I didn't have sisterly thoughts at first…*fuck*, at all. But we can't. My mom is happy for the first time, and I can't fuck that up."

I sober at that. I can't fuck this up either. Dad is so happy. It would break my heart if I did something stupid, like hooking up with my future stepbrother— If Dad marries Kate, that is. Either way, Asher is off limits.

"If we are being all honest here, I thought you would be an asshole too."

He points to his chest and gasps dramatically. "The fact my mom is dating your dad? Or that I'm just soooo good looking?"

I burst into a giggle and shove him back. He stumbles but rights himself as he continues to chuckle.

"You think very highly of yourself, Asher. Who says you're good looking?"

Asher scoffs, the smirk on his face never leaving. "I will have you know, my mom tells me that all the time. So, it must be true."

I like Asher. He's funny, and yeah, good looking. If his mom wasn't dating my dad, I would probably hook up with him at a party. But that won't ever happen now. But I'm glad, because I can see us being good friends.

"Come on, now that we've established the no-fucking-each-other rule, let's eat ice cream."

He stands there, looking at me in surprise. With a laugh, I grab his tee and pull him toward the house. When we get to the front door, he pauses. "You're going to be a handful, aren't you?" There's no mistaking his grin.

"Yeah, but you know you're gonna love it."

ELEVEN
JACE

"The fuck?" I mutter to myself as I watch Mila out my window with some guy who'd just driven her home.

My bedroom door slams hard against the wall in a loud thud. I spin to see Grady standing there in only his gray sweats, his hair still damp from the shower he took when he got home tonight. He was out with Makai—who tutored Grady in algebra—after practice. No idea why they needed to start first day back. Maybe they're friends now.

I'd come straight home. I'm going to confront Mila... demand to know who was first. Yeah, it's fucking with my head now. It's all I can think about, and I need to stop.

When those girls came up to me at lunch and told me I was Mila's first kiss, happiness swelled inside my chest. I tried to push it down—I didn't want to hurt my best friends—but I was ecstatic.

Then Mila shook her head, and I realized she was fucking with me.

My fists clench at the memory. I'd wanted to go over

and demand she tell me I was first in front of everyone. But I'd looked over to Roman, and his face told me everything I needed to know about how he felt about not being first. And then there was the way Hunter remained quiet, not even joking with the girls or flirting like he usually did.

They wanted to be first as much as I did. Neither wanted to be second. And no one wanted to be last. If they found out they were last, it would hurt them in a way they could never come back from. I know I wouldn't be able to come back from that.

"The fuck, Grady?" I ask as he strolls into my room like he was invited in.

"I could say the same to you, *fucker*. Mila's back, and apparently you knew. Hell, I had to find out the gossip at practice today."

We both had practice after school, but he'd been off with the defense doing their thing. Technically, I'd known since Friday she was back...I just hadn't wanted to tell him.

I shrug and roll my eyes at him.

"Oh, shit," Grady snaps beside me as he glances down at Mila. "No fucking way, that's Mila?" He gives a low whistle. "She grew up, and she's looking damn fine from here." He nudges my shoulder with his.

"No, she doesn't. She's a lying bitch," I grit out between my teeth.

Grady laughs as he places his hand on my shoulder, and I tense under his touch. "I heard about the kiss thing, man. That shit is tough. I wonder which one of you boys she picked first?"

Him and everyone else on the planet is wondering the same thing.

I turn away to peer out the window again. My view is clearer now, and I recognize Mila talking to a Lakeview Prep asshole. I grind my teeth together.

"Is that"—Grady moves closer to the window—"Asher Rossi? Oh fuck, it is."

I look closer and, sure enough, it's the wide receiver for the Lakeview Kings.

"She's dating a King? No wonder you're pissed. You've loved her since you could talk, and now she's back home and with a King."

I shove him away from my window and close the blinds. I can't deal with this shit, not now. Grady is having a field day with this, biting his knuckle to keep in his laugh as he bounces on his toes.

"Nah, I'm sorry, man. That sucks. I shouldn't laugh. That shit is all kinds of fucked up."

I don't reply. I just want him to leave. Let me spiral in my fucked-up head and heart. In the last four years, my heart wasn't a factor, even with Britney. When Mila left, she took it with her. But Mila is back, and my heart is damaged now. I hate that I still care about her. I hate her for that.

"I'll drive her to school. She can watch me at practice every day, and I'll take her home." He flexes his bicep and winks at me.

I shake my head, letting the rage settle. Grady shouldn't be this excited after seeing Mila with Asher. Grady is one of us—he's a Rebel. "Get out." I shove him, and he backs up out of my room. I kick the door behind him and hear his deep chuckle when Mom yells out not to slam doors.

She'd asked me earlier about helping Mila out. But

there's no way I'm driving Mila to school. She can ride her bike or some shit.

Grady and I are eleven months apart. He calls me Grady 2.0, and for most of my life, I've been considered the copycat. It's hard not to be when you're so close behind in age. All the regular shit you do growing up, I did it a year after him. What did he expect, for me to never walk and talk?

Football, though, that's where things are a little different. I'm QB1. I've wanted that position since before I could run, and I never thought it would happen until I finally had a growth spurt during freshman year. Grady's rough and naturally aggressive. He's a linebacker for the Rebels. I'm all about the offense, and he's all about the defense.

The thing is, growing up, Mila was all about the defense too. So they would spend a lot of time talking football. I used to hate it. I told my dad that Grady was stealing my best friend, and he would tell me it wasn't true. They just had some things in common, and I had to let her be friends with other people. It had been hard to share her with Hunter and Roman, and the last thing I'd wanted was to share her with my brother too.

Grady heard me complaining to Dad, and he and Mila ganged up on me and tackled me with tickles. I hated to be tickled. They'd done that a lot. I'd been small for my age. But I'm not now.

I grab my phone and bring up Hunter's number. He answers after only two rings. "You ready to go now?" he questions. I know he's talking about Roman, but that's not why I'm calling.

"No, haven't heard from Roman. This is worse. Mila is fucking a King, right now."

I hear a strangled sound and a cough to clear it up. "You sure?"

"I just saw her and Asher Rossi. She grabbed his tee, man, and dragged him into her house."

Hunter starts cursing while I open my blinds again. I can see right into her room. The blind is drawn, but there is a small gap, and I see movement in there.

"Oh, fuck, I can see them in her room."

"Fuck, stop it. You were pissed at me and Roman over the kiss shit, which is total bullshit because you kissed her too. We agreed not to talk to her, then today she called you out on that stupid rumor, which could have ruined any chance at college for us all. Now you're stalking her? You need to get over her. Come on, I'll meet you at The Shed in ten. Not gonna wait on Roman."

I grunt and hang up. The Shed is where Roman spends most of his nights. It's an underground fight club, and he fights there regularly. Hunter and I don't like it—it's shady as all hell, and we only go there to drag his ass home after a bad fight. He said he was going tonight.

I think back to school and how Mila fucked with his head. Tonight would be bad.

The only way Roman expresses his feelings is on flesh. He makes good money fighting, and he needs it. But it's more than that. Fighting is his release.

That didn't make us feel any better about it. Going down there scared the fuck out of me and Hunter. The Shed is full of motorcycle clubs and gangs. We warned Roman to be careful, not to mess with any of them. But I don't know if he's mixed up in that or not. He never speaks about it.

There were times we had to pick him up after Arthur called. He's the old guy who runs things down there. He would call us up to collect our boy because he'd go too far. Roman never lets us take him to the hospital, but fuck, there have been times when I sat awake for days to make sure he was still breathing.

Times like that, I bring him here. I'm glad Mom and Dad are out of the house more now. They're gone most weekends, letting me and Grady fend for ourselves while they take mini vacations. It works out great for me. I can have parties at our place most Saturdays.

I grab my keys and shrug on a black hoodie as I make my way downstairs.

"And where are you going?" Dad asks.

I stop with my hand on the door knob. "Out with Hunter and Roman."

"It's late. Can't it wait until tomorrow?"

I shake my head. "Nah, Roman's dad is being an ass. I need to make sure Roman is good until he passes out."

Mom comes around the corner, her hand on her chest. "Tell that boy to come here. You know he can stay here anytime. I get so worried about him living with that man. That man isn't a father—no father treats his son that way."

"I'll let him know, Mom." I kiss her cheek, and she smiles lovingly up at me as she pats my cheek.

"You're a good friend, Jace."

No, I'm not. If I was, Mila wouldn't have stopped talking to me. She would be here, hanging out with me like old times.

But now she's in her room, sucking a King's cock to make me angry. This is the end for me. There's no coming back from that.

I hate Mila Hart.

TWELVE
MILA

I walk outside my house, unsure how I'm getting to school. I never heard from Ella about who would be driving me. I know, deep down, it won't be Jace. Still, a part of me is holding out hope.

I notice movement out of the corner of my eye and turn to find Grady running toward me as he hollers my name. Wrapping me in a bear hug, he says, "Holy shit, you're back. I didn't know. I had all this extra stuff I had to do yesterday, but today I'm all yours. Tell me all about New York, about yourself. You have really grown up, Mila."

My cheeks heat at his words.

Grady pulls away from me and looks at what I'm wearing. Once again, I'm in jean shorts and a tank, which is showing off some nice cleavage. His eyes pause on my neckline before raking down to my bare legs. It's gonna be a hot day.

"You're my driver?" I point to a white sedan on the street, assuming it's his car.

"I drew the short straw. Sorry, Mimi, you get me today."

My ears catch on the old nickname. He's the only one to ever call me that. I hated it when I was younger, but now I can't wipe the grin from my face.

"So, I got football training after school, like always, but I finish at six. If you have something after school, or you wanna wait around and watch me pump weights and run drills"—he wiggles his brows at me—"you're more than welcome to stay."

I tap my finger on my chin, as if I'm really contemplating it. "I don't know...that's not very enticing, a bunch of sweaty guys and their big muscles sounds *boring*," I jest with a wink. "Do any of these practices end up with you tackling Jace and putting him on his ass? Because if so, I'm so in."

Grady lets out a huge laugh. "I'll see what I can do, Mimi."

The ride to school isn't long enough to catch up, but it's still great. I'm mostly grateful Grady isn't pissed at me. We don't talk about Jace, just about football, his parents and their romantic weekends, and how sad his love life is.

Which is hard to believe. He's attractive, and I'm sure he's exaggerating that his love life is sad while, in reality, his sex life is on fire. Because there's no way girls don't throw themselves at him.

There's a guy waiting for him when we pull up. His bag is slung over his back, and he's wearing cute black-rimmed glasses. He's not a football player, but he's obviously friends with Grady.

"Makai, meet my neighbor and old friend Mila. She just moved back from New York."

Makai, who is cute in a nerdy way, gives me a small smile and wave. They walk in with me, talking about some Xbox game they both have; I haven't a clue what they're saying but they obviously enjoy gaming with each other. They leave me to go to their lockers.

I'm floating as I walk to my locker and find it on the first try. I almost cheer, happy I studied the map this morning over breakfast. I'd just grabbed my books and closed my locker door when I feel the air change around me.

"You're fucking a King?"

I spin to see Jace, Hunter, and Roman behind me in the hall. Their seething expressions causes me to press my back against the locker. I've never seen them like this before.

What the hell are they talking about, fucking a King?

"Asher James, wide receiver for Lakeview Prep Kings." The way Hunter spits out *Kings* makes the hair on the back of my neck stand up. His eyes flash with anger.

"You should have gone to Lakeview. You can't be here and fuck with a King," Jace warns me, and that's when I notice we have an audience.

Is he for real? Why would he even think...oh, fuck. "You're spying on me." It's more a statement than a question.

Jace crosses his arms over his wide chest, and a few students make sounds like they're scared. What, like Jace is gonna hit me? He might be angry, but he would never hurt me. Not physically, at least.

"It's hard to miss you and Asher cuddling up in your driveway." He cocks his head as if to challenge me to tell him he's seeing shit that isn't true.

I burst out laughing. It's not gonna make a difference what I say. He's made up his mind that I'm sleeping with Asher. They all have.

Jace clenches his teeth, and I swear I can see the steam

coming out of his ears from the way his face is a deep shade of red. He's mad.

And me? I turn and walk away.

This doesn't warrant an explanation. If Jace and the others want to think that, let them. I'm not going to correct them today, or any day. He thinks he saw something and jumped to the conclusion I'm fucking Asher.

"Hey," Hunter calls out.

Raising my hand in the air, I flip the three of them off and walk to my first class, ignoring everyone around me.

◀▣▶ ◀▣▶ ◀▣▶

Ugh...lunch.

It's too bad Grady and I don't have the same lunch period. I would've happily sat with him. Instead, I'm once again staring at my three former best friends and the very disgruntled girlfriend of one.

God, Britney really seems to have it out for me. I've done nothing but show up here. I haven't attempted to take her man away and have no intentions of doing so either. But if she's gonna go all classic mean girl, I'll have to make sure she doesn't mess with me.

I sit down with people I've seen in some of my classes. Today they don't move away, so that's a good start.

"Hey, I'm Mila." I decide to play the new kid and attempt to make a few new friends—hopefully non-asshole ones.

"I'm Sadie. We have World History together."

I smile over at the girl opposite me, who has a genuine smile on her face. She has purple hair too. Looks wicked. "It's nice to meet you, Sadie," I say around a mouthful of fries.

"This is Cadence." She gestures to the red-haired girl beside her.

The color isn't natural, but it's gorgeous. I've never attempted to dye my hair. It's such a light blonde, I'm worried I'll hate the color and won't be able to get my natural hair back. A hairdresser told me once that I would need to be one hundred percent confident if I tried color it, as my hair will si=uck that colour it and I wont be able to go back.

"Is it true that you—"

I put my hand up quickly to stop the rest of Cadence's question. "If it's about sleeping with anyone, it's not true."

She nods and then looks over to the football table. "Sorry, I just always wanted to know what Hunter looks like naked."

I almost spit my food across the table. Both girls raise their brows at me as they started laughing.

"Sorry, Cadence doesn't have a filter sometimes," Sadie says around her giggles.

Shaking my head, I laugh with them. "Nope, I get it. He is hot…a hot asshole. But I get it. I have seen him naked, though."

Cadence and Sadie swing their heads back to me and move in closer, wanting to know more.

"Seriously? Was he, like, big?"

I laugh again. "He was eight, and I screamed. His mom came running in like someone had been murdered."

like sleepovers with Hunter, because his mom has a big bathtub. Every time I stay over, she fills it with bubbles, and it's the best. Then, she brushes my hair, but I don't need that today. I'm big enough to brush it myself.

I put my warm pjs on and grab my hairbrush out of the bag Daddy packed for me. I haven't seen Hunter. He's probably getting ready in the other bathroom. So, I go back to the one with the big bath.

Hunter is standing naked in the middle of the room.

I can see his penis and his balls. I scream at the top of my lungs because I don't know what to do. He screams too and hides himself behind his hands. But it's too late. I saw it all. My hands fly to my eyes, and I try to unsee it. But I can't.

Boys' parts are so weird. I know they have different parts to girls, but it's so freaky how they hang there. I haven't even seen Jace's parts, and we sleep over a lot.

"What's happened, what's going on…oh, god."

I open my eyes, and Hunter's mom freezes in the doorway when she sees us. She gasps and grabs us both by our arms and takes us back to Hunter's room. She then looks at Hunter and shakes her head. "Mila, love, let's wait outside for Hunter to change."

My dad and Hunter's mom, Angela talk for a while the next day, and afterward, Dad talks to me about sex. He tells me that boys have a penis and girls have a vagina, and together they make a baby. I have soooo many questions on how, and why.

I have to promise Dad I'll keep what I know a secret. I'm not allowed to tell anyone, because it isn't my job to do so. Only their parents tell them when it's right and they're old enough. That's a secret I have no issues keeping.

"That's so weird that you knew them before…like, before they were popular," Cadence says.

I hadn't thought of it that way. It's not weird to me. But, looking back, maybe it was weird that I was the only girl in the group back then. I never had other girl friends to go out with or ask to stay over. It was only the guys.

Over the rest of lunch, we talk about New York, clothes, and the new season of *Stranger Things*.

The bell rings, and we all get up.

"Same time tomorrow?" Sadie asks.

"Sounds great to me."

THIRTEEN
MILA

F riday. I've been back a whole week, and Mom hasn't called. Not even once. But I can see from her social media that she's been making the rounds, showing off her baby belly. Well, lack of one, since it's too early.

I'm lucky that Cadence and Sadie took pity on me. They've been driving me home every day after school so I don't have to wait around for Grady. He's still giving me a lift in the mornings, but he gets home way later than Jace at night. Yeah...I've been spying out my bedroom window.

One thing's for sure—Jace, Hunter, and Roman haven't spoken to me once since the whole Asher thing. I told Cadence and Sadie who Asher is to me, that I'm pretty sure my dad will marry his mom. They think it's funny that I haven't told the guys. But what's it to them? They chose to believe the worst because of what Jace saw. That's on them.

Just one class left for the day, and I'm free for the weekend. Madison and I are going to the movies tomorrow. We're having dinner at their place tonight, and I'm curious to see their home. Dad said they have a hot tub. Not that it's hot tub weather…not yet, anyway.

I groan when I get to the locker room and see Britney and Summer. Why am I taking P.E. again? To torture myself?

Since I'm a great runner, I thought I might try out for track. I'm also kinda lazy, so maybe not.

"Sluts aren't welcome here," Britney sneers. Summer laughs like the comment was actually funny. These girls have no idea how to be mean girls. Hell, my school back in New York was full of them, and they were scary. These two are harmless imitations.

"Then, why are you here, Britney?"

She sputters. "You wish you had Jace, but he's mine. I see the way you look at him. If you get too close, I'll hurt you."

I sigh. Honestly, if they weren't so pathetic, I'd play along with them longer. But it's just too tragic to watch.

"Okay, Stink-ney." That got a few curse words from the two of them.

I get changed and stroll out to see the three of *them* are in class with me. Now that I'm closer to them, I notice that Roman has a black eye. He catches me looking and turns away. Fuck, is that from his dad? I want to ask Roman if he's okay. I want to offer to let him stay at my place.

But he hasn't spoken to me, even in class. Next week, we need to start class projects, and he's my partner. So I need him to at least talk while we're trying to work. He can go back to ignoring me, or whatever this silent shit is, after our project is complete.

Jace steps up to me, his arms crossed over his chest as he cocks his head. Wow, he wants to talk to me now? Okay then, I'll bite.

"What?" I question, mirroring the same position, knowing my arms are only making my boobs look bigger. He looks down at them, and I can see his intake of breath as he licks his lower lip. Fuck, having him look at me that way has my tummy flipping. It's a heated look, one I don't think he realizes he's doing.

"Who was first?" he whispers, his eyes now burning holes into mine.

I raise my brows. Are we still on this? This line of questioning is getting old, especially after he accused me of sleeping with a King on Tuesday and ignored me all week.

"Who did I kiss first?" I ask.

Britney chooses that moment to slide into his side, catching onto what Jace just asked me. "Yeah, I know it wasn't Jace. He would never want to kiss you."

I laugh. Is she serious? "Dang, you're a little slow, Britney."

She puffs up her chest and holds Jace tight. "And what do you mean by that?"

I throw my hands up. This girl is unbelievable.

"I don't know, the fact that your boyfriend is asking me which one of him and his friends I kissed first? He's the one asking, Britney. Wanting to know if it was him."

Her mouth pops open and closed again as her cheeks grow pink.

Jace's jaw ticks. "It doesn't matter," he growls and moves to turn away.

I sigh. I fucked this up. It's my fault I got myself into

this mess in the first place. I hate this, the silence, the mean words. He deserves to know, they all do. But I could never hurt them with the truth.

"I get it, okay? I know I fucked up. I thought I was leaving forever, and I kissed you all. I was twelve, and I felt like leaving you was the end of the world. To me, you all were my first kiss, no matter the order it happened. The first kiss I had with each of you was my first *with you*. And I'm sorry if you can't accept that answer, but it's the only one I have to offer."

The real answer would hurt two others, and I could never live with myself if they found out who my first was. I can't hurt them again. I did this, I made my bed, and I had to be the one to apologize. I deserved the cold shoulders, the silent treatments. Everything they had done was understandable. I hurt them all.

Roman is walking away. Did he hear me? I hope he did. Hunter looks at me now, really looks at me. He nods and turns to follow Roman. My heart starts beating faster. I want him to understand and let me back in, I just miss them all so much. This past week has been hard.

The past four years have been hell.

"They think we're fucking?" Asher bursts into laugher.

"Hey, asshole, you would only be so lucky to be tapping this." I smack my ass as I turn around in his room, looking at his trophies.

"I was cockblocked from the get-go. I guess I should be grateful to be tapping that ass in rumor."

I shake my head at him and laugh. I wonder what Jace saw that made him think I was with Asher. We hadn't done anything that would make someone think we were more than just friends.

"Damn right. But if I was you, I'd watch my back next Friday. Rebels versus Kings. Gonna be an amazing game."

It's all everyone has been talking about, the first game of the season. The schools are rivals, and even though I love football, I don't get caught up in all that shit. It's the game that excites me.

"Who you gonna cheer for? Me or them?"

I turn to him and tap my finger on my chin.

"Or your dad," Asher adds. "He's been an amazing coach."

"Mmm…tough decision. I love my dad, and you're okay, I guess." He pouts, and I chuckle. "They didn't speak to me for the rest of the day, so I don't think I'm in their good graces…yet." I poke my tongue out at Asher when he rolls his eyes. "I guess I can wear blue…might fire them up and help us Rebels to win."

Asher flops onto his bed. "You're playing with fire, woman, and I'm only too happy to stoke it. Just to watch the Rebels burn." He rolls off his bed and goes into his wardrobe before throwing a ball of blue fabric my way. "It's a spare…and has my number."

I hold up the navy blue jersey he gave me, the number thirty on the back. It's big—I'll be swimming in it—but I grin.

Maybe I'll wear it. If *they* don't speak to me all week, then I will. To support family…and maybe it will make Jace so angry that he'll speak to me. I'll have to see.

"So, stepbro, are there any parties tonight?"

He grins. "I thought you would never ask. Wear that, and we'll go." He points to the jersey in my hands.

"Only this?" I arch my brow.

He rolls back onto his bed and groans. "Tell me again why we can't make these rumors true?"

FOURTEEN
HUNTER

Roman spits blood at my feet, and I jump back.

"Hey, what the hell?" My shoes are white Air Force sneakers. "If I wanted red shoes, I would have bought red ones."

But he isn't looking at me. He's looking at his opponent in the ring. I fucking hate this place. But Roman actually asked if I would come down tonight, and I couldn't say no. He needs me, and I'll always be there for him when he calls. Just like he is always there for me when I need him.

"We have a game tomorrow. Do you really think this is the best idea?"

I know no matter what I say, he won't listen. Once he gets an idea in his head, he goes through with it.

His glassy eyes tell me that, for him, this is the best idea. His dad was drunk earlier, and Roman called me for help. He's spiraled again.

I need him to snap out of it, and Jace isn't here to help me. I have no idea where the fuck he is, but I need him now. Because I have never been able to break Roman out when he gets like this.

"Come on, man, let's go. We can still get some food at Annie's."

He looks right through me, and I know nothing I say will change his mind. Not until he's knocked out. He never just walks away. He will fight until there is nothing left to give.

I grab my phone and call Jace again. Roman moves again and swings at the huge fully-grown man he's been fighting the past ten minutes. I'm surprised they are still fighting, to be honest. Roman is messed up from last night still, and I won't be surprised if he has more broken ribs after this.

When Jace doesn't pick up, I scroll to Mila's name. Is this still her number? If I call her, will she come? Would she even be able to help Roman? He hasn't spoken about her at all since that first Saturday we saw her. He still hasn't spoken to her in chemistry, not even about the projects we're now starting. I would swap with him, if I could. I would partner with Mila.

I wanted to talk to her last Friday. I know what she said was right. She isn't here to hurt us or break us up. She could, very easily, with the truth, and she won't. What she said was perfect—we were her first kiss. Each of us. I don't care how it happened. She was my first kiss, regardless, and all week I've wanted to get her alone so I could talk to her. But between practice and school, Mom's drinking getting worse, and Dad working late, I haven't found the time.

My thumb hovers over her name. Will she even pick up if she sees it's me? I rake my hand down my face. I look over to see Roman on the floor and the ref counting. Fuck. He's out cold. I shove my phone in my pocket and jump in to get him.

Arthur is there beside me as we drag him out of the ring. Roman's eyes flutter open, and he grunts something as he tries to get up.

I push him down. "No more, you're done. How many fingers am I holding?" I put two fingers in his face, and he swats them away.

"Boy, no more. Okay? You have a football game tomorrow, and you're gonna be hurting pretty bad after Tommy knocked your lights out," Arthur growls at him.

Roman settles back, and I sigh in relief. I'm not cut out for this hellhole. I hate it here; I hate what he does. But if I don't accept his fighting, he'll try to hide it. Hell, he already hides more things from me and Jace than we realize.

I saw the leather prospect cut at his trailer earlier. He's prospecting for The Sons of Death MC. I didn't tell him I saw it. I need to talk to Jace about it. I'm scared for Roman more than ever.

Is it Mila that tipped him over the edge, or has he already been pursuing this behind our backs? He has a motorcycle. He's had it for a while now. But I never thought he would join a club.

My phone goes off, and I see it's Jace. I answer with a sigh of relief. "I need you, now."

"This is it, boys. Let's start this season off by showing those Kings who's best." Coach Perkins holds his clipboard as he looks over us. The locker room is abuzz. We've been waiting for this day.

"Lakeview has been working hard, but we've been working harder. How you feeling, Roman?" Coach looks him over, and Roman just nods as he taps the side of his helmet.

He looks like shit, but Coach would never tell him that. He's here, like me, for the love of the game.

I don't feel much better than Roman looks. I hardly slept. I was worried he'd broken a rib and it had pieced his lung or something, not to mention he'd snored loudly when I brought him back to my place.

Coach rambles on about defense, and Grady pounds his chest. "Hell, yeah," he cheers.

The whole locker room grows loud with the rest of the team cheering Grady on. The team loves him—he's the glue that keeps us all together. Our captain. He is going all the way. There are college recruiters out there tonight just for him, and he received offers last year. But he's holding out for the right one. He won't tell us which one that is. I hope he gets the college of his dreams. He's a four-star recruit, so I would say the odds are high he will.

"Rebels, bring it in," Grady calls out. We bring it in, our hands all reaching toward the middle as Grady calls out, "Work hard, play hard, and victory is ours."

"Victory is ours," the room erupts.

"Rebels on three. One! Two! Three!" Jace calls out.

The room echoes with the stomping of feet and the cheers of my fellow players. We all run out onto the field. The Rebels' stadium is full. A sea of red and blue surrounds us, with fans cheering their respective teams. A home game is the best way to start the season. And against none other than our rivals, the Kings of Lakeview Prep.

Nothing beats the feeling of running out onto that field. I don't think I'll ever be able to explain it. It's something you have to experience firsthand—the crowd, the anticipation, and the atmosphere. Everything about playing under the bright Friday night lights.

The cheerleaders scream our names as we run past, Emerson lapping it all up. I guess he's over the whole Mila thing. Not that he even had a chance with her.

I jog along, stretching as I do. I look up into the stands since Mom said she would come tonight. Dad said he had to work late. I've come to not expect him at my games. As long as I keep my grades up, I don't see him. I can't see her, but I hope she's out there.

There is one blue among the sea of red, and as soon as I see her face, I stumble to a stop, Emerson crashing into me.

"What the fuck, dude?" he curses. But then he looks to where I spotted her.

She smiles and waves at us, but I can't see past her blue jersey for the Kings. She's actually dating Asher Rossi?

I shake my head, unable to believe it. She really is. Jace had said so, he saw it. But I had hoped deep inside she wasn't. That he made a mistake. She turns to the girl beside her, and I see Asher's number.

"Holy shit, she's with a King, for real?" Emerson croaks. "I thought that was a bullshit rumor. She never told me."

I shove past Em, not caring if she told him or not. I need to find Jace, now.

I run my finger over the scar on my palm, and my eyes narrow on Asher from across the field where he's warming up.

Gritting my teeth, I growl out to Jace.

"He's a dead man walking."

FIFTEEN
MILA

Kate and Madison picked me up to take me to the game. Dad and Asher went with the rest of the players, so it was just the three of us. We had a meal at Annie's Diner, and it was nice. Just the girls. I got to know Kate more, and she's amazing. At first, I'd assumed she's like my mom. That she'd married someone with money and lived that housewife life. Nope, Kate is successful in her own right. She owns her own business, selling cake supplies to bakeries around the country.

I respect that about her. Her ex—Madison and Asher's dad—is a corporate lawyer. He lives out of state, so he wouldn't be coming to any games. I feel bad for Asher that his dad won't be here for his first game of the season. Madison told me he's an asshole, and she hasn't seen or spoken to him in over a year.

Kate asks me to sit with her and Madison when we get to the stadium, but I tell her I have friends waiting for me. I don't, but I can see how uncomfortable Madison is being so close to three girls that are standing there watching us.

The looks they give her rile me up, but I don't want to cause a scene or make it worse for her.

She's still having issues with her best friend, Bella. I'd hoped things might have gotten better for her, but they haven't. So, I ask her if she wants to sit with me, and she jumps at the chance. Kate's face lights up at my offer, and she tells us to have fun and meet her at the car after the game.

"This is so exciting," Madison screams in my ear from where she sits beside me in the stadium.

Ridgecrest has a decent field—nothing like Lakeview's, of course—but it doesn't matter to me either way. All that matters is the game the guys are about to play.

Madison isn't wearing her school colors; she's in a black tee, jeans, and a baseball cap. When I first saw her in the car, I'd pointed out her lack of school spirit. She pointed out my own, and I laughed. I'd chosen to wear Asher's jersey. If the guys think I'm fucking him, might as well dress the part. I'm being a bitch, but I don't care.

Wearing the rival team's colors makes me more of a rebel. A few people tell me I should fuck off to the Kings' section, but then they see who I am and start to whisper loud enough for me to hear. They can't believe I would wear this jersey after I fucked three Rebels players...that maybe I've moved on to the other team.

This is how rumors and gossip spread. I don't care. They can say what they like. I know who I am. No use wasting my voice on people who don't care what the truth is. They only care about the drama. High school will end, and none of this means shit in the real world.

I'm glad to have Madison's company, since it means I'm not here alone. Cadence and Sadie said they have better things to do than watch football. As much as

Cadence wants to see Hunter naked, she's not obsessed with him enough to attend a football game.

The Rebels run out onto the field, and the crowd goes wild. I can feel the excitement buzzing in the air. Madison laughs and looks at the people around us.

"Have you ever been to a game?" I ask. Asher told me he was on the JV team as a freshman, but she acts like this is all new to her.

She shakes her head and chuckles. "I kinda hate football. All sports, really. I would rather be home reading a book, so I've never come to one. I usually beg Mom to leave me home every time Asher has a game."

I smile and nudge her shoulder. "What changed your mind tonight, then?"

She smiles over at me and says, "You."

My heart stutters a little. She came because I'm here. I reach my arm around her shoulder and give her a side hug. "I'm so excited you're here. It's gonna be fun seeing you react to the game for the first time. Watching the game in person is totally different. You get swept up in everyone cheering and booing. Even if you don't like sports, you'll get into it. I bet you'll be cheering by the end of the night."

The players start stretching and warming up as they practically parade in front of us. Hunter is there, and when my eyes catch his, he stops suddenly. Emerson runs right into the back of him.

I smile and wave at Hunter. He hasn't spoken to me all week. But he also doesn't seem as angry anymore. I've been hoping we could talk so I can explain who Asher is to me. But we haven't had the chance.

"Who's that?" Madison asks as she stares down at Asher and Em.

"That's Hunter, one of my former best friends. And the guy beside him is Emerson."

"Oh, Hunter looks angry."

She isn't wrong. I realize he saw Asher's number on my back when I turned to look at Madison. But, hey, if he looks to the other side of the field, he'll see Asher's mom wearing the same jersey. Not that he'll look over there or that it matters. It's the fact I'm the one wearing it.

If Asher hadn't insisted I wear his jersey, I would feel bad for him. He's gonna get his ass handed to him with the way Hunter is eyeing him already. I just lit the fuse…I hope Asher can handle the explosion.

"This is gonna be a fun game." I chuckle sarcastically.

It doesn't take long to realize the whole Rebel defense is after Asher. As soon as our offense leaves the field, Asher walks on with his confident swagger. Then he looks up at me and points, tapping his hand over his chest.

Madison waves, and I shake my head and wave back. I can't wipe the smile from my face, cocky bastard. Asher loves it. He's riling them up, and they're taking the bait. I can only hope he doesn't get hurt for his antics.

I watch as the Kings' center snaps the ball to their quarterback, Walker Murphy. I met Walker last weekend at the party Asher took me too. He's good. Hell, he's better than that. He's going places.

He looks down for the pass, and Asher is running at an amazing speed. But I see Grady and two other Rebels on him. Walker passes to another player, and the Kings score their first touchdown.

It isn't good for the Rebels, since they are running defense in a way that leaves pockets open. The fact that they have it out for Asher is letting Lakeview score touchdowns easily. I'm starting to regret my choice of clothing…

Asher has been sacked a few times, and the last time he limped a little. I did warn him.

Jace catches my eye from the sideline. I don't see anger on his face. I see...jealousy? No, that can't be right. He's just pissed I'm wearing Asher's number. He all but ignored me this week. And Britney has still been trying to mess with me in her PG, friendly-mean-girl way. It's sad but enjoyable to watch.

I wave at Jace as he walks onto the field. I watch him put his mouth guard in as he turns to me, calling out the next play. The center snaps him the ball and Jace passes it down the field to Hunter, who catches it. I start jumping and screaming. It's an amazing throw by Jace, but Hunter is amazing too. I didn't know what to expect when I saw them play, but they are unreal together.

Hunter is sacked almost as soon as he catches the ball, and they set up the play again. I can't sit down. My throat is hoarse from screaming. The score is twenty-one to twenty-eight, and we need this touchdown and a two-point conversion to win. This is such a close game, my nails are digging into my palms. Even Madison has started cheering for the Rebels. The crowd around us has turned her into one of us. I laugh because she doesn't really know what's going on, but I love her newfound passion for football.

Hunter sprints down the field toward the end zone. The way he moves is magnificent, dodging the Kings' defense and twirling as he looks back to Jace.

But the pass to Hunter is fake. My eyes have been so focused on Hunter that I miss Jace passing the ball off to Roman, who is now barreling at full speed down to the end zone. I'm jumping up and down with the rest of the crowd. Holy shit, he's going to make it. We are going to score a touchdown.

At the last moment, a Lakeview player tackles Roman. But it's too late. Touchdown. The crowd erupts into cheers.

"Holy shit, Mila," Madison shrieks. "Look at the score."

I look over to the score board, already knowing what it will show. With less than a minute left, the Rebels need those two points to win.

My heart is pounding as the ball is snapped to Jace and he spins, looking for an open player. He dodges King players and darts around. Roman is open, and Jace throws to him. I hold my breath as a King tackles him. Roman holds his hand out with the ball as he goes down. But I can see from here he didn't make it. The refs give the *no* signal, and the crowd's mood changes instantly.

"Fuck, so fucking close," I mutter to myself. The Kings are good. But if our defense had tightened up more, we could have won this.

The Kings take a knee and that's it, first game of the season over.

As we leave the stands, Madison smiles and grabs my arm. "It was such a good game. I didn't really like football, but now I get the appeal." She wiggles her brows at me, and I chuckle.

I swing my arm around her shoulder as the crowd starts to move forward. I don't want to lose her. "Hey…it's not about the hot guys." She tilts her head at me, and I shrug. "Okay, maybe a little."

I'm sad for the Rebels, but I'm happy for Dad and Asher. First win of the season. They're going to be on cloud nine when we see them.

. . .

meet Dad, Kate, and Asher out by the car. They are coming back with us. Dad has a huge grin, and Asher is talking to a few cheerleaders, who giggle and bounce at his every word. He looks over at me and winks. I roll my eyes at him but grin. He just chuckles and goes back to talking to them.

"Dad." I hug him and pull back. "The team was amazing. All the work you've done with them has paid off."

He kisses my head and chuckles deeply. "Ah, they were great before I started there, but thanks for the confidence boost, Mila."

"Where's my favorite girl?" Asher calls out as he approaches me, his arms wide open to hug me.

I shove him, and he stumbles back, laughing. "You were amazing, Asher. But I'm not hugging you in public." I get closer to him, bringing him in as if I'm going to whisper something. "People might think I know you or something." I yell as I pull back and give him a disgusted face.

He laughs and dusts off his shoulders then poses like a body builder. "As if you're that special to know me." Clearly, those two touchdowns he scored have gone to his head. But I love it.

Then he becomes more serious. "Thanks, Mila. I could hear you cheering me, and you too, Madison. Does that mean you two will be at all my games?" His grin is contagious as he raises his brows.

Madison shrugs, and I follow suit.

Seeing Asher's gaze on something behind us, I turn to see what he's looking at. Hunter, Jace, Roman, and Grady are watching us. I look back to Dad and Kate, and they're holding hands, kissing, and appearing very much like the couple they are. I wonder if the boys can see what a stupid mistake they made in assuming I've been fucking Asher.

"Grady was out for blood today," Asher says. "And he isn't even one of your boys. I'll be feeling it once the adrenaline wears off."

I shake my head at him. "I told you this wasn't a good idea. Plus, Grady…he's kinda my friend. He's been driving me to school all week, so I think he might be mad at me now."

I didn't think about that when I put this jersey on. But if I have to catch the bus, it'll be worth it. The looks on the guys' faces are priceless.

"Let's go, *sis*. There's a Lakeview party calling our name."

Dad kisses his girlfriend before opening the passenger door for her. I sit in the back of Kate's white BMW SUV next to Madison, but my eyes are drawn to where I last saw the boys. They're gone.

Probably off to a Ridgecrest party…or to drown their sorrows. They lost by one point. If I was them—or with them—that's what I'd be doing.

SIXTEEN
MILA

Lakeview sure knows how to throw a party.

I drove Asher's BMW here—he told me it was his dad's gift to him, and he doesn't want it. "But, fuck it. Free car."

He'd wanted to call an Uber like last week, but I prefer to be in control of when I leave. And volunteering to be the designated driver isn't exactly a sacrifice. I haven't touched alcohol or anything since I've been home, and I don't want to go back to that.

In the New York party scene, I was always in a drug haze and never myself. I did stupid and reckless things. I was out of control. But now that I'm finally back home with Dad, I don't want to mess things up. It's like I have a second chance at life, and I refuse to waste it.

I still love to party and dance, but with drinking off the table, I make better choices. I don't find myself without my underwear in a strange bed or jumping into a pool with all my clothes on.

I take a deep breath and repress those thoughts.

"Miss Mila Hart. You here to spy?" Walker Murphy asks me grinning widely. He leans lazily against the kitchen counter.

I lean over and cup my chin in my hands as I lean against the other side of the counter.

"Spy? Never. I'm partying with the winners tonight."

"Hell yeah, girl," he cheers loudly, his red Solo cup full of beer raised in the air, and a bunch of guys whoop in response.

When I met him last week, he had no idea who I was. Asher thought it would be funny to see which guys on the team tried to pick me up, and Walker was the first one to try his luck. He'd flirted hard. I'd enjoyed the attention, I'm not gonna lie. But as soon as Asher mentioned my dad, I became untouchable, and any guy who'd seemed interested kept their distance. Except for the cocky quarterback.

Walker said he was still game if I was, and I'd laughed. "I'll ask my dad if it's okay. I'm sure he won't mind the star quarterback fucking his only daughter."

He'd laughed and raised his hands in defeat. "Well played, Hart. Well played."

We seem to have fallen into a friendship as easily as I did with Asher. They have a lot of similarities. They work well together on the field and are great friends off it.

I prefer to dance and have a good time. I wasn't looking to hook up last week, and I'm not now. Asher seems to be enjoying himself with a blonde girl in the corner; I think she's one of the cheerleaders I saw talking to him in the parking lot earlier. He did tell me to leave him behind if I can't find him when I'm ready to go…he might be *busy*. I have no intentions of cockblocking him.

Or breaking up the celebration with Little Miss Thang over there.

Asher catches my eye, I nod and give him a thumbs up. He raises his cup to me in a toast. I really love having Asher as a friend. Once we relegated our relationship to the friend zone, it's been so easy to be around him. Yeah, every so often there's a bit of sexual tension. But it's more the fact that we can't than we actually want to. The forbidden fruit. Our parents aren't engaged or married, so it's not wrong if we take a bite from the apple. But I don't want that to happen, and I can tell he doesn't either. So, the mutual agreement works well.

As the night wears on, party people disperse. Some guy keeps trying to dance with me, and I tell him, repeatedly, to leave me alone. He isn't on the football team, but he's a senior at Lakeview. So, I guess the whole "my dad is the assistant coach" doesn't scare him away.

Eventually, he gets the hint, and I'm left to my solitude. I take a mouthful of soda from my red cup and look out at the huge yard from the deck. I'm not sure whose house this is—one of the players, most likely—but, man, the twinkle lights hanging in the trees and shrubs really give off a romantic vibe. Everyone out there, kissing and dancing, laughing, and just being free and young, makes me smile.

My stomach hurts a little, but I push the ache aside and drink more from my cup. Someone throws a girl into the pool and there are cheers all around. I laugh and feel light-headed. What the hell? I ate earlier, but maybe I need some food.

I look at the couple kissing beside me, and they start to blur. I rub my eyes, and they aren't in focus anymore. My stomach lurches. Oh shit, I think I'm gonna be sick. I stumble back inside. Holding the wall, I peer down a hallway that's moving. Why is it so wonky? I'm just looking for the bathroom.

I feel a hand behind me, leading me.

I try to see who it is, but they hold me close.

I try to push away, but I can't. They're too strong.

"Are you okay? I'll help you," says a male voice that's familiar. Is it the dancing guy?

"No," I slur, trying to move away again.

"Jessica, where have you been? Get over here."

My arm is yanked, and I don't know who Jessica is... Is she Jessica? She leads me somewhere. The bathroom. I stare at the bright white tiles and throw up.

I feel something cold on my face... I'm on the floor... and the tiles are cool against my warm skin. How did I get here?

"Hey, do you have someone I can call? You're either drunk, or you've been drugged. We need to get you home."

"Drunk?" I croak out.

I didn't have anything but soda. I feel heavy and strange, and my body is so warm. I open my eyes to my fingers, and I can't get them to move right. They feel like they aren't even on my body. I need to get my phone... Where is it? In my pocket? My jeans...I have jeans on. I feel the girl slip my phone out.

"Who do you want me to call to come get you?" I hear her talking to someone outside the bathroom. The voices are low, and the people speaking are confused about who I am.

Who am I?

"Who do we call?" another voice asks. She pushes my hair behind my ear. I close my eyes and picture him. The person I need, the only one who can help me.

"Jace."

Then it all goes black.

SEVENTEEN
JACE

Everyone's off at Emerson's house. I'm not. I'm home. We lost. By one fucking point. Fuck the party. And fuck Mila for wearing that fucker's jersey to the game.

My game.

Mom and Dad went to bed long ago. They're off early tomorrow on some mini vacation. Again. Not that I blame them. If I worked as hard as they do and finally had some money saved for traveling, I would too.

The controller in my hand vibrates as I get shot. They get me again, and I die. I curse and throw my Xbox controller on my bed. It bounces off and lands with a thump on the floor. I can't even play Fortnite without thinking about Mila and all the shit that happened tonight. I throw myself back against my mattress and run my hands through my hair.

I'm blaming her for our loss. Grady was pissed when he saw her wearing Asher's jersey. But when Asher pointed to Mila and tapped his chest, it set Grady off. He was enraged. I'd never seen him like that before. He had it out for Asher, and he sacked him harder than needed. More than once.

It surprised me. He'd been so happy to drive Mila to school all week, boasting to me about it every day. Like they have some little secret club that I'm not a part of. I told him to stop spending time with her, that she's dating Asher Rossi. He didn't believe me.

But seeing her wearing Asher's jersey, that pushed him over the edge. Hell, it pushed me, Hunter, and Roman over the edge too. Mila distracted all of us from the game.

Roman slipped up after he watched her in the stands. It was easy to spot her wearing the navy blue of the Kings.

Hunter ran two seconds late after looking over at her. It almost cost us the play, but he caught the ball only to be sacked at the same time.

They were angry and pissed. I was too.

Until we left the locker room to see James Hart, assistant football coach to the Lakeview Kings, Mila's dad and my neighbor, kissing Asher's mom. Asher's mom was making out with Mila's dad.

My mouth had dropped open. I'd realized my mistake too late.

Hunter shoved me. "You said she was fucking him. Looks like, from here, that she's gonna be his new sister. They don't look like they're together. What did you see?"

What did I see? She touched him...she pulled him to the house...they were laughing. That's it. Looking back on it, I'd assumed there was more to it, but it was an innocent exchange. There was nothing to suggest she was with him. I'd fucked up.

"I thought there was something."

Hunter had believed me when I told him that she was

fucking a King. He said didn't want anything to do with Mila when he found out, which made me ecstatic. I didn't have to worry about how he felt about her and the pact.

As soon as Mila got into the car with her dad and the Rossi's, Hunter turned to me, his nostrils flared. He gritted his teeth and let out a strangled sound. "I'm... fuck!" Hunter shoved me again, and I stumbled back a step.

"Fuck, Jace, I'm so mad right now. I believed you when you said she was fucking him. I was happy Mila was back, you knew that. And you put that shit in my head. You fucking lied. Was it because you didn't want me to have her? Were you that worried I would break the pact again? Just like you and Roman had?"

I didn't know what to say to that, so I didn't say anything. Was it because, deep down, I knew he would break the pact? That he would choose her over me?

Did I want her to choose me, and with Hunter and Roman out of the picture, did I think I would have a chance?

I didn't know if I'd wanted to believe she was with Asher to stop the others from forming something with her again, or if I'd really believed it was true.

"I'm going to Emerson's party. I don't want to see you right now."

Hunter didn't give me a chance to explain. He walked away from me before I could even come up with something. What could I say?

Roman grumbled something and left with him.

Grady drove me home. He didn't speak to me the whole way. I tried, but he wouldn't talk to me. As soon as we got back, he changed and left for the party.

In one night, I upset my two best friends and my

brother, all because I thought I saw something that turned out not to be true.

I'm relieved Asher and Mila aren't a thing. But why the fuck did she wear his jersey? To teach me a lesson for calling her out on it at school? When she'd laughed in my face that day, I should've realized something didn't add up. Mila isn't the type of girl to take my shit, and she didn't even correct me.

Have I pushed her too far? I hadn't been able to see past my anger long enough to see what's been going on in front of my eyes.

My phone goes off, and I sit up. Rolling over the messy sheets, I pick it up from my side table. I expect it to be from Roman or Hunter. They normally call me this late if they need me. But I'm surprised to see *her* name there.

I clench the phone tighter. She is the reason I'm here and not off at some party. She got into my head and is fucking with it. Every day at school, those legs...her mouth. Fuck, I want to kiss her so bad. Shove her up against her locker and bite that pink lower lip into my mouth. Brand her as mine. Grind my hard cock against her wet pussy and show her how hot and crazy she makes me.

Then, the next moment, I want to push her away and tell her to fuck off. To go back to her mom. *Leave*. Leave me again for another four years without a word.

"What?" I growl into the phone. What is she thinking, calling me at almost two in the morning after everything that went down tonight? She knows she got into my head. Fucked our play up, and we lost the game.

"Ah, is this Jace?" a strange female's voice asks on the other end.

I sit up straighter, my anger dissipating, replaced with

concern. Why would some chick be calling me from Mila's phone, unless she's in trouble?

"Is Mila okay?" My throat feels tight as my heart speeds up.

"No, she asked us to call you. We think some asshole drugged her."

A chill wraps around my body at those words. *Drugged*. I growl in anger, at the fucker who did this, at myself for pushing her away.

I jump to my feet. "Fuck." I rake my trembling fingers through my hair as I search for my car keys. I look down at my loose tee and gray sweats. My feet are bare. Socks... fuck the socks.

"Where is she? What's the address? I'm on my way."

The girl rattles off an address in Lakeview. My fingers shake as I log it into Google Maps. It says it will take me twenty minutes to get there.

"I'll be there in ten."

I've never experienced this feeling before. It's as if I can't breathe. My throat is constricted as I grip the steering wheel, willing my car to go faster and for no cops to pull me over.

Someone drugged Mila.

I rub my hand down my face. I need to snap out of it and be in control for this. I pull onto the street. There are cars everywhere; there's nowhere to park. I dial Mila's number, grateful I never deleted it and that it's the same number as four years ago. Like mine.

The same girl answers. "Hey, you here?"

"Yeah, gonna double park out front. Can you come get me?" My hands are shaking. Why are they shaking?

"On my way."

I hang up and get out of my car. She'll be fine; she's the

strongest girl I know. She's Mila fucking Hart. But then, do I really know her? The new her, the girl she is today? I don't, and fear sets in. I glance around the property. This place is a mansion.

A girl with long, dark curls waves at me from the double front doors.

"Jace?" she asks, and I start jogging, my heart lodged in my throat when I see her worried expression. "Come with me. We saw her acting all drunk, and a guy was leading her into a bedroom. We took her from him and he ran. She vomited then passed out, but not before she told us to call you. We don't know who she is. She's not from Lakeview."

I shake with rage. Some asshole drugged Mila and was going to rape her. But I need to focus on one thing right now—Mila.

The girl leads me down a hallway. The house is mostly empty, since most the party is out back, and I recognize that it's a football party. Of course. They're celebrating their win over us. But where the fuck is Asher? She wouldn't have come to a Kings party without him. That's why she's here and not at a Rebels party.

She's also here because you made sure no one would want her at a Rebels party.

I walk through a doorway and into a bathroom. It's huge, like the house. The small, crumpled form of Mila on the floor has me frozen. This isn't the Mila I saw hours ago. It breaks my heart to see her so weak and vulnerable. I take a small step forward then stop. I don't know what to do here. How could someone do this to such a beautiful soul?

I'm so out of my element. The once strong and sassy Mila is lying unconscious on a bathroom floor of a house in Lakeview, at a Kings party. If you'd asked me four years ago what I would have seen in my future, this wouldn't have made the list, ever.

I crouch down until I'm on my knees, and the cold tiles tell me this is really happening. This isn't some bad dream. My hands hover over her face, her body.

"Mila? God, Mila." *I'm so sorry*. God, I'm so sorry.

She doesn't respond. I gently bush my hand over her cheek.

"Wake up. I'm here to take you home." She is warm to the touch. That's a good sign, right? But her breathing seems shallow.

"It's me, Jace." When she doesn't move at all, I reach for her throat and feel for a pulse. It's steady. *Thank fuck*. I stand up and rake my hands through my hair as I pace.

"Fuck," I scream out.

The word echoes around the tiled room. This is all me. I did this. If I had just asked her why Asher was at her place. If I hadn't kept pushing her away.

Wanting to know if I was her first kiss had messed with my head so much that it consumed me. I glance back down to her still form and slam my fist into the tiled wall.

"Are you Jace Montero?"

I turn to see another chick in the bathroom with us. I hadn't seen her when I first came in. I don't answer her. I don't want the Kings to know I'm here and start shit. Mila needs me. That's all that matters right now.

I reach down and scoop Mila into my arms. I cradle her close to my chest. Her head flops onto my shoulder. One of her hands falls, and the girl with the curls picks it up and places it in Mila's lap. She then hands me Mila's phone, and I hold onto it best I can as I take Mila out to the car.

"Thanks, I got it from here."

The girls both hesitate at the front door, but I don't

want them to follow me. Mila is safe with me; I have her. I'm glad I didn't lock my car before coming inside. I was so preoccupied when I got here, it hadn't crossed my mind to lock it. I reach for the door handle with her in my arms. Mila's head lolls back, and I gently shuffle her in my arms. She's so small and barely weighs a thing.

I look down into her face. Her mouth is parted, and she's breathing fine now. I wrench the door open harder than I need to, but she doesn't wake.

Leaning into the car, I place her in the passenger seat. Her hair is over her face, and I brush it away. She lets out a small moan.

"Hey, hey, sweetheart?" Her head rolls forward, and I push it back, brushing the hair from her face again. Her eyes flutter open and her brows furrow as she looks at me. I haven't been this close to Mila in years, and she is truly beautiful. Always has been.

"Jace?" she croaks.

My shoulders sag in relief. "Yeah, I got you, Mila."

She smiles at me, and my heart bursts in my chest at the sight. But then she lurches forward and vomits…on me, in my car, and some on herself. I catch her hair before it gets on that. Fuck, shit. I should've brought something in case that happened. It was only a small amount, at least. She probably threw most of it up before I got here.

"Mila?"

She closes her eyes and groans before passing out again. When I hear voices coming closer, I tilt the chair back and quickly fasten her seatbelt. I close the door and round to my side. I glance over and see a few King players talking in the front yard, they haven't seen me yet. I need to get out of here before they see me and Mila.

I slide in and study her. She's making little sleeping

sounds… I don't think she needs a hospital, but she needs someone to take care of her. In case she gets sick again. It's probably for the best she vomits up whatever she was given.

I'll take care of you, Mila.

EIGHTEEN
JACE

t takes almost thirty minutes to get home. I drive like an old lady. I don't want to jostle Mila or make her vomit again before we get home.

I carry her up the stairs to my room, lay her gently on my bed, and look at her small form…in my bed. There's vomit on her jeans and her tee. I can't leave her like that. But I also don't want her to think I'm a fucking creep either.

"Mila? Mila, I need you to get undressed. So I can get you some clean clothes."

"Mmm…Jace, huh?" she whispers as she tries to sit up. She grabs her stomach, flopping back onto the bed with a groan. "My tummy hurts." She curls into herself, and my chest pangs with guilt. I need to stop blaming myself right now. I need to take care of her.

"Do you want me to help you? If you give me permission, I promise not to look while I help take your clothes off."

"Mmm…okay."

I take that as all the permission I need. This isn't

anything other than me helping her. I unbutton her jeans and slide them down her long legs. For someone so short and petite, she has legs for days. But, as soon as the thought enters my mind, I look away, as promised. I chuck her jeans on the floor and focus on her top.

She has rolled over. I catch a glimpse of her pink thong and the smooth skin of her ass. *Fuck.* I stare at my ceiling as I reach for the hem of her tee and lift it off. She isn't much help, and I have to wrangle her arms out. But once the tee is off, she curls into herself.

I quickly turn. I'm worried she'll fall off the bed if I leave her, so I look around my floor for something to put her in. I snap up one of my jerseys. It has my number and name on the back. It's dirty, and a deep part of me wants her in it, wearing my name and smelling like me.

I slip it over her head and get her arms in. She rolls, sprawling out like a starfish, and mumbles my name. I look down at her, her blonde hair a mess over my pillows. Her breathing is even, and she makes this cute snoring sound.

Seeing her in my shirt, on my bed like that, has my cock hard.

Yeah, I'm a sick fuck. But at least I admit it.

I ignore my cock and pull off my vomit-soaked sweats before slipping into bed beside her. I cover her up with the sheet and watch as she sleeps. She looks so peaceful. Her eyelashes are dark and long, something that has always fascinated me with her almost-white-blonde hair. Her cheeks are tinted pink and her lips parted as she sleeps.

I can't stop thinking about what could have happened to her tonight if those girls hadn't stopped the fucker who did this. I'm going to find him, and I'm going to kill him.

◗ ◗ ◗

hear my alarm, but I put it on snooze, hoping it won't
wake Mila. I can't leave her here alone. She needs me.
Coach will understand. I slip back to sleep, but it
doesn't take long for Grady to open my door without
knocking, looking for me.

"Fucker, what the hell, you're still in bed… What the?"
He looks to the pile of blonde hair beside me and takes a
step toward my side of the bed. He peers over, and I hold
my hand up and shake my head.

"Don't wake her," I whisper.

I watch his facial expression change when he realizes
who is in bed with me. His jaw ticks with irritation. I know
what's going through his mind, because I would have the
same thoughts if I found her in one of the guys' beds. He is
angry, confused, and concerned.

"What's she doing here? In your bed, of all places," he
spits out through gritted teeth.

I shake my head and run my hand through my hair.
"I'll tell you the full story later, but I picked her up at a
Kings' party. Someone drugged her. They tried to…" I
can't even say the words out loud.

But Grady is filling in the blanks as all the color drains
from his face. "What the fuck? Who?" he growls, and Mila
shifts, groaning as she moves closer to me.

I reach out to hold her hand, and she settles again.
Grady is still as he stares down at Mila. He storms out of
my room without closing the door. I watch Mila's face. She
is sleeping again. I don't want her waking up and feeling
like shit. I want her to sleep it all off before she wakes up.

Grady returns with a glass of water and two aspirin.
He places them on my side table before looking over at her

sleeping form. His face softens as she makes a small sigh, and he looks at me.

He shakes his head and throws his hands up. "You should have called me. I would have come. The whole team would have come and smashed the fuck out of the asshole who did this." He doesn't wait for me to answer. He runs his hands over his face then points at Mila. "I will tell coach there's an emergency," he states, before leaving the room and closing the door softly behind him.

Mila mumbles something, and I move closer to comfort her. She starts tossing and turning in my arms, and she sounds frightened. "No, please. No."

"Mila, Mila? You're having a bad dream. Wake up." I hold her close to me, and she stops. Her body slowly relaxes, melting in my arms as I hold her close to my chest.

"Jace?" she asks, and I freeze. She's awake.

Is she going to be upset with me when she discovers that she's in my bed, wearing my top and just her underwear?

I hum back to her in response, hoping she'll fall back asleep. I'm not ready for her to leave my bed yet. I want to keep her here forever.

Where did that thought come from? Fuck. But it's true. I don't want to let go of her. Not now. Not ever.

"You're warm," she mumbles as she presses her body against mine. Her thigh slides over mine, and she fits perfectly beside me.

My cock is now awake and very aware of how close she is. But she doesn't seem to notice my reaction. I look down and see that she's fallen back asleep.

Fuck. Mila Hart is going to be the end of me.

NINETEEN
MILA

Something hard and warm is pressed up against my back. My head aches as I crack an eye open to a dark room. Only a slither of sunlight peeks in, enough to tell me this isn't my room…and isn't my bed.

Hell, this isn't even my house. Is it Asher's? A room I didn't see? He said there were six bedrooms in their house, and I only bothered to check out his and Madison's.

But that doesn't explain the warm body spooning me. Is it Asher? Oh god, please don't be Asher. I shuffle forward, and my bare legs swish against the sheets. Fuck, shit. I grasp at the fabric over my chest. I'm wearing a top. One that isn't mine.

I hear a deep groan beside me. Asher? I don't remember a thing from last night. Football, Asher, party… I can't.

My stomach hurts and my limbs are weak. I blink and see aspirin and a glass of water sitting out for me. I sit up a little and take them. I down the whole glass of water, the liquid soothing my dry throat. I feel a little lightheaded and groan as my head hits the pillow. I roll over, hoping the person beside me isn't a guy...even though I know it is.

I see dark brown hair—it's all disheveled from sleep—a strong jawline, and light stubble of facial hair. His lips part, and he lets out a small snore.

Jace Montero.

Holy fuck. How the? I sit up and scan the room. My head pounds at the sudden movement, and I can see I'm in his room. Not a lot has changed in four years, except a poster of a girl in a bikini on a red Corvette and football trophies that I haven't seen before.

Why the hell am I in his bed? How did I even get here?

I need to pee, so I slowly extract myself from his bed without waking him. He's wearing a white tee, so he isn't naked. That's a good sign, right? I peer at the huge top that's down to mid-thigh. It's red and has *Rebels* emblazoned across the front. I'm wearing his football jersey.

I roll my eyes. I have no idea how I got here, but this—I pull at the fabric—is interesting and not how I expected to wake up today.

I sneak down to the bathroom, hoping Ella or Daniel don't see me sneaking out of their son's room. I quickly do my business and wash my hands. I look at myself. My makeup is smudged and my eyes are bloodshot. I wash my face and drink a little more from the faucet. I put some toothpaste on my finger and quickly finger brush my teeth to get the bad taste out my mouth then gargle with mouthwash.

I'm feeling semi-human as I sneak back to Jace's room. I look around on the floor for my handbag. It was in the car last night. I left it in there, so I could come home if I wanted to. But I don't see it. I look around for Asher's car keys and find them in my jeans pocket. I scrunch my nose up at the stain on my jeans. Omg, did I throw up?

I'm so confused, but I try to focus on what I remember. Dancing, the fairy lights outside. Feeling sick. I was sick, and there was a girl...Jessica? My head pounds, and I don't want to wake up Jace. I don't know why I'm here or how, but I'm hurting too much to fight with him right now.

My body sways, and I know I just need more sleep. I crawl into the bed, as far away as I can from Jace, and cover myself. I close my eyes. I will get up soon and sneak home... Dad might have a hidden key somewhere, and I can get in.

hear someone speaking softly, and I want them to be quiet. I roll away from the voice, but I don't open my eyes. I don't wanna get up. Just let me sleep in. I'm too hot, though. The sheet is stifling. I roll onto my back and reach for the hem of the shirt, and I shuck it. But it's not enough. I throw back the sheets and sigh as the cool air of the room hits my heated skin. I feel better already.

My muscles are achy, so I stretch my arms up and arch my back, letting out a yawn. I hear a groan from beside me and freeze.

I just realized where I am. Holy fuck. I roll my head toward the sound and open my eyes slowly. Two big chocolate eyes stare back at me.

Jace. I suck in a breath.

He puts his phone down beside him, never looking away from me. He must have been talking to someone on his phone.

He doesn't speak. He just watches me. I notice then

that he isn't wearing a shirt. He had a white one on earlier, and now he is only in blue boxer briefs.

I slowly lower my arms and his eyes fall to where my chest rises and falls rapidly. I'm in my pink lace bra and thong that I put on last night. Tension stretches between us. It's like a thick sexual fog has landed over us.

My skin prickles when he licks his lower lip. My heart speeds up, and I bite my own lip to stop myself from moving. It's like I have been caught in a spider's web, and if I move, he'll eat me.

Do I want him to eat me? I rub my thighs together, aware of how wet I am. The desire builds, and I let out a small moan as sparks light up my body. Jace rubs his hand down his smooth chest and abs until he's cupping his erection over the thin fabric of his boxers.

He strokes himself a few times over the fabric, and I watch, wanting to reach out and touch him. I want to feel how hard he is for me. I want him to feel how wet I am for him. I run my fingers over my breast, his eyes following my every movement. I dip them down to my belly then over the lace of my thong. I'm soaked as I tease my clit, arching my back and softly gasping at how aroused I am. *Fuck.*

Jace groans as he presses the heel of his palm into his erection. The sight has me working harder. I rub myself until I can't stand it anymore. I slip my fingers under the fabric of my thong, and my fingers find my clit again.

I moan as the feeling spreads through my body. It won't take long for me to come like this. I keep up my assault on my clit, working myself higher and higher. Closing my eyes and arching high off Jace's bed, I gasp. The rush of my orgasm is so intense, it almost shocks me.

When I open my eyes, Jace has freed his cock. It's long

and hard as he strokes it. At first, the strokes are slow as he twists his fist on the up strokes. But when our eyes meet, the strokes become faster and jerky. I lick my lips and look down at his hard length. The head of his cock is shiny with pre-cum, and I reach out to him.

He stops and watches as I run my finger over the top of his cock. I'm greeted by more pre-cum and the strangled groan of Jace. I look over and see him watching me. He's so tense, his muscles all bunched up and tight. He's a beautiful sight and not one I was expecting to see. I bring my finger to my mouth, and he watches, his mouth parting, as I suck it in, twirling my tongue around so I can taste him.

His abs clench tight, and he groans deeply as ropes of cum spray onto his taut stomach, over and over until he shakes and lets out a deep sigh before sinking into the mattress.

We still haven't spoken a word; we just stare at each other. Like, if one of us speaks, it will break the spell. I don't want that. I don't think he does either. All I can hear is our rapid breathing and the beat of my own heart.

But the spell is broken by the sound of footsteps, and before we can do anything but turn, Jace's door swings wide open, slamming against the wall. Roman is standing in the room, looking down at us, breathing hard.

Oh, fuck.

TWENTY
MILA

J ace is the first to break the silence. "It isn't what you think."

But from the look on Roman's face, that isn't very believable. I turn to see Jace has pulled his boxers up, and he's cleaning himself off with the white tee. He holds his hand out to Roman to keep him from running. Toward him, or away from him, I don't know. But my heart hurts. This isn't how I wanted this to happen. I never planned for this to happen.

Did I want it to? Yeah, but I held the same feeling and attraction for each of them, equally. I just wanted to be their friend again. Had I hoped for more? Yeah, maybe, but I'd never pick one over the others if they all felt the same way.

"Roman?" Hunter calls from downstairs, and Roman turns, stomping out of the room.

Fuck. I scramble off the bed. "Roman." I run after him, but he's down the stairs before I can catch him.

I follow, finding that Grady has stopped Roman, who is pacing at his side. I rush down the stairs and hold my hands out over the front door. He can't leave like this; he's angry and upset, and I can't have this on my conscience.

I've already fucked up enough with him. I need him to understand I'm not abandoning him. That what he just saw...it doesn't mean... *Fuck*, I don't know what it means, but I can't lose him like this. I know he'll never forgive me if he walks out that door before I can explain.

Roman pauses a moment. His eyes, dark and stormy now, pin me to the door from across the room. His fingers twitch as they rake through his shaggy hair, the long strands catching and giving him a sexy, messy style that I itch to run my own fingers through. But I know this is the wrong time to be thinking about that or doing it. This isn't how I thought my day would start...end... I have no idea how I'm even here.

"Roman, what's wrong?" Hunter asks from the corner of the room.

Grady is standing beside Hunter now. They look to me, and I realize I'm still only wearing my pink lace underwear. Fuck, I can't go back and grab something else. Roman will leave. I need him to stay, so I can explain.

"Roman, it's not what you think," Jace calls from the top of the stairs.

Roman lets out a guttural cry. I can feel it in my chest, the pain he's experiencing. I'm begging him with my eyes to stay and wait until we can work this out. He starts toward me, and I press myself against the door, my hands down by my sides, hoping I can hold it if he tries to pull it open.

"Don't leave," I plead.

Roman moves swiftly, toward me, and his gaze lowers to my body as his arms come up beside my head, caging me in. We are close...so close that I can see the small, faint scars on his face. Like the one from the lake when he declared he was Tarzan and swung. Landing in the water at an odd angle, he caught a tree branch under the water and cut his face.

"Roman?" I whisper, my fingers trembling now.

My heart is racing, and my breathing quickens as he stares at me like he doesn't know what to do with me. I lift a hand to his face. My fingertips hover close to his jaw. I'm not touching him, but he isn't pulling away. I can see the other three just in my vision. I sense this isn't something Roman normally does. But I'm not worried about him hurting me. I'm worried about me hurting him.

I break the barrier between us, running my index finger along his brow and down his sharp cheekbone. He doesn't blink. His eyes bore into mine as he breathes rapidly. They are full of anger and hurt.

His head tilts slightly. He's studying me, as I am him. I continue my exploration of his face as I run my finger along his lower lip, and his tongue darts out to where I just touched. Like he's tasting me. I shiver.

His breathing deepens, as though he's trying to breathe me in.

He drops his gaze to my breasts, my chest rising and falling fast and my nipples hard against the lace. Every breath I take sends pleasure to my core. I rub my thighs, wanting friction there again. I'm so wet and achy. I never knew just one look from Roman could make me feel this way.

His right arm falls away from the hardwood behind me. I'm worried he'll run, but he surprises me when he wraps his huge, calloused hand around my throat. The rough texture feels amazing against my delicate skin as he presses me into the door even harder. I suck in a breath as the other three guys take a step closer. They haven't spoken, but they are watching us closely.

His forehead touches mine, and he inhales deeply as he closes his eyes. I arch my body into him. I want him against me, to show him how he makes me feel. But, before I can, he crushes his hot mouth against mine. I gasp, reaching up to his hair and pulling him closer. The hand on my throat tightens, and I let go of his hair, running my hand down his back he grips tighter.

I start seeing stars dancing in the back of my eyes as my skin prickles all over from the lack of oxygen. The feeling is intense, everything is heightened, and I can feel every brush of fabric and his hot breath against my skin. I drop my hand to my side, and he loosens his grip, but only enough that I won't pass out.

No touching. I understand the warning.

His kiss is vicious, but I take everything he has to give as he claims me. His body presses hard against mine, and I flatten my palms against the door to stop myself from touching him. I can feel how hard he is all over, his cock pressing against my belly through his shorts. I press myself into him, rubbing myself against his hardness.

He groans and pulls back, his eyes clear now. His hand still grips my throat as he breathes heavily. It's like he realizes only now that we have an audience. I almost forgot, myself. He spins and sees the three others standing there.

He staggers away from me, his hand dropping, and I instantly miss his touch. He lets out a strangled roar and runs to the back door.

I let out a ragged breath and slump against the door. I'm cold without Roman's touch, and with Hunter and Grady staring at me like I'm some kind of circus freak, I feel vulnerable and naked. I never let myself feel this way. I never want to feel this way in front of anyone, especially them. I choose strength every day I wake up. But now…I know I need to be strong, so I can brush off any insults they throw my way about what just happened.

Except, I can't always be strong. Sometimes, I have to let my guard down and be seen. And right now, I want to be seen. I want them to see that I'm hurting without them in my life.

"Are you okay, Mila?" Hunter is the first to come to me, his hands hovering over my throat.

Jace runs to the back door, but the action is delayed, like he's chasing after a ghost. Unsure if he wants to catch it, but he doesn't want to let it get away either.

"Yeah, I'm good. Just need some clothes." I shiver under his gaze.

Hunter takes a step back and yanks his tee over his head. I lift my arms as he puts it on for me. When my head pops out and I brush my hair back, he smiles down at me. The soft fabric flops down to the middle of my thighs.

"What the hell was that?" Jace questions as he walks over to me, looking over me the same as Hunter just did. I think he is asking himself more than me, because I'm just as clueless about what happened

"Roman kissed me?" I reply as the silence stretches out, unsure if it's the right thing to say.

Jace lets out a strange laugh and runs his hands through his hair. He isn't looking at me now. He's in his own mind.

Hunter wraps his arm around me and leads me over to the couch. "Yeah, but…Roman never kisses?" He sounds like he's unsure if it's a question or a statement.

"He did then." I chuckle lightly, trying to break the

tense atmosphere in the room. Grady brings me a tall glass of water, and I take it from him with a, "Thanks."

"Mila, are you really okay?" Grady asks me, and I nod. I can still feel where Roman's fingers held my throat. I never thought I would like something like that, but I do.

"I have never seen Roman kiss, hug…hell, even touch a girl," Jace says. "I questioned his sexuality once. I just wanted him to know that it was okay if he likes guys. That he was my friend either way. I didn't want him to have to hide that part from me if he was, you know?"

My mouth drops open. He's never seen Roman kiss a girl? Because, holy hotness, that kiss was epic. There is no way he hasn't been kissing…someone.

"What did he say, about the guys?" Because that kiss certainly felt like he's into me. I could feel how much he wanted me.

Jace shakes his head and chuckles. "He shoved me and grunted that he likes girls. Told me to leave him alone."

Everyone laughs at that. That sounds just like Roman. The old Roman, at least. The new one, I'm only starting to scratch the surface, and I have a feeling there are many more layers to Roman Valentine.

"He doesn't like people touching him. At all. He never lets us touch him, even a pat on the back after a good game. He flinches away."

I'd touched his face…but he didn't let me touch his hair or body. He made that very clear when he squeezed my throat tighter in warning.

I'm surprised no one has asked what set Roman off in the first place. I guess, with me down here in my underwear and Jace in boxers, they could guess something happened.

Roman had caught me with Jace.

Hunter, Jace, and Grady had watched as Roman kissed me like I was his last meal.

And now Hunter has me curled up against him, Jace sits beside us, and Grady is watching us like he's the fourth wheel.

I shake my head. It's too early in the day to wrap my head around this. I'm hungry and exhausted. I need to go home, shower, and change. Get freshened up. I clear my throat.

"I broke your pact. *Again.*"

TWENTY-ONE
ROMAN

have fifteen missed calls from Hunter and Jace. It's not unusual to have that many, but usually I'm in the ring smashing some asshole's face in when they're calling. Tonight, I've watched every single call on my phone since I left, ignoring them all.

I put my cell in my pocket and listen to the buzz of the tattoo gun. I watch as Ronnie tattoos a butterfly on some chick while her friends stand nearby, giggling and taking selfies. They keep looking over, trying to flirt with me. Everyone wants a turn with the "bad boy." I've heard it time and time again.

"Hey, you, come here."

I shake my head, and two of them pout at me. "Fucking hell," I mutter to myself. Why did I come here? But I know the answer already. *Mila.*

I have no idea why I ran... *Fuck, I ran.* I never run from anything. I smash it, destroy it, until it's not in my way. But I can't do that with Mila.

I kissed her. I kissed the girl I have been in love with since I was six. I can't ever do that again. I can't let her get under my skin like that and let go. Because if I do, she will get hurt. I can't ever…

My phone vibrates in my pocket again, and I pull it out to see Grady's name on there. Great, they're involving him now. I turn my phone off and slide it in my pocket. I don't want to talk to any of them. I don't want to see their faces, and I don't want their questions.

I run my hands down my face, trying to forget the way she smelled and how she crinkled her nose at me. How her lips tasted, how she kissed me back…how she touched me.

No one touches me.

Yet, I let her touch my face. Her touch was so light, a caress along my lip. I wanted to suck her finger into my mouth and taste it. I wanted to show her how hard my cock gets for her. I groan, my cock hardening even now at the thought of her gasp on my lips, her throat gripped tightly under my hand.

I don't know what came over me when I kissed Mila. Fuck. My knuckles tighten and my hands ball into fists. I need to fight someone right now, but I know The Shed is the first place Hunter and Jace will look for me.

When Grady told us that Mila was at his place and that someone drugged her at a Kings party last night, I lost it. I wanted to kill the son of a bitch who did that to her. I was out for blood, but Hunter suggested we go see her.

After the revelation last night that Mila and Asher Rossi aren't together, Hunter claimed he wouldn't speak to Jace again. He was angry at Emerson's party, so much so, he didn't even hook up. And, normally, Hunter is the type to hook up at every party. He always has a girl hanging off him.

The girls keep their distance from me. That's the way I like it.

I'd freaked out as soon as I got into Grady's house. He said she was fine and in Jace's bed, but I'd needed to see with my own eyes she was safe. That she wasn't hurt. When I threw the door open and saw her pale, smooth skin bare, and the pink lace of her bra and thong, I lost it.

I didn't want to scare her, but I wanted to kill Jace just as much as I wanted to kill the fucker who drugged her. I could smell sex in the air; I'm not stupid. The fact that Jace wore a guilty expression, and he was trying to wipe the evidence away as if nothing happened, told me all I needed to know. Even if they didn't have sex, he broke the pact.

He's the one who goes on about the pact every day, that we can't let her back in because she will be the end of us. Yet, he breaks it the first chance he gets. He wants her for himself. He doesn't give a shit about what I want. Or Hunter. Since she left, it has been all about Jace. He's become a selfish asshole. And we let him.

"Hey, Valentine. Think you can help this lovely young lady out with a butterfly?"

I look up and see the brunette that was taking selfies is now standing beside Ronnie. He winks at me, and I let out a deep breath. He knows I hate these airheads, but money is money. I stand up and nod, pointing to the chair beside Ronnie's.

"Your name is Valentine." She looks up at me, batting her fake lashes, and I grunt in response. My last name is Valentine, but I'm as far as you can get from a romantic. I don't do flowers and hearts.

I do pain.

"Love, Valentine here don't talk much," Ronnie drawls. "But he's the best. He'll take care of you."

I shake my head but don't look over at him. I've known

Ronnie for years; I've been escaping to his shop since I was a kid. The art of tattoos has always intrigued me. I'm not great at drawing, but if you give me the design, I can tattoo that onto any skin.

I didn't come here to tattoo today, but Ronnie has been teaching me for years. He thinks I'm decent enough with a tattoo gun that he now pays me to work in his shop. I enjoy it, too. He mostly gets me to tattoo college girls who venture in here on the weekends.

"I like the quiet ones." She smiles up at me as she pushes down her skirt, exposing the virgin flesh there. "I want it here," she says, pointing to her hipbone.

Another stupid butterfly on a hip for a college chick, coming right up.

It doesn't take long. A small butterfly on the hip is nothing. I might have smiled when she cried out in pain. I have done dozens of these in the last month, and I never get tired of hearing them complain that it hurts. You get a tattoo on your hip bone—what do you expect? It's gonna hurt.

The shop's door opens, and I look over and immediately roll my eyes. Hunter walks into the shop with his cocky swagger. He's wearing his glasses, not his contacts. I'm surprised since he hates his glasses. I haven't seen him wear them at all this year. He used to wear them for reading when we were younger then high school he had to wear them all day. Now, he wears contacts all the time.

When he sees me, he nods. Like he knew I was here the whole time. "Hey, Roman. Been trying to call you." He leans against the counter, and the chick I just inked sidles up next to him.

Hunter catches her gaze and gives her his panty-dropping smile. I ignore him and get the aftercare pack ready so she can leave with her friends, who are all standing outside, giggling.

"Hi there. I'm Ruby, and you are?" She puts her hand out to shake Hunter's, and he chuckles, reaching out to her.

"Well, hello there, Ruby, I'm—"

I cut in and jam the sheet and aftercare cream into her hand. "He's sixteen and about to leave."

Her mouth drops open. I don't know if it's at the shock of his age or that I've spoken to her for the first time. She pulls her hand back and grips the aftercare to her chest.

"Hey, fucker." Hunter shakes his head at me, a smile still on his lips as he turns to her. "What I lack in age, I make up for in skill."

Ronnie laughs at that. "Yeah, yeah, Mr. Ego. Use your lines somewhere else."

I chuckle, and Hunter shakes his head, because his lines do work. Just not on college chicks. Ruby leaves and I turn to Hunter, who is staring at me like I just grew another head.

Fuck. He's here about the kiss. Fuck, that was more than just a kiss. I devoured Mila in front of them all. They've never seen me lose control like that. Is Hunter angry with me?

"What?" I finally ask.

If he is here to tell me he hates me now because I kissed Mila, he can say it and fuck off. I know I fucked up. Sometimes I sense that because I don't talk as much, that they think I'm stupid. I'm not. I watch, I wait, and I see shit others don't.

He is quiet as he watches me. I look out the front and see his red Audi. Jace doesn't seem to be with him.

"We got a name."

I quiz my brow at him. *A name?*

"The fucker who drugged Mila."

I growl. That fucker is gonna pay for what he did to her. He'll be lucky if I leave him breathing when I'm through with him.

"Come on. Shit's going down, and I thought you would want in."

Hunter knows me well. I always want in. That guy will never walk again after I'm done with him.

When we pull up to the restricted area behind the old warehouse downtown, near my place, I'm surprised. But not as surprised to see Jace's car there beside a white Beamer. Does that belong to the fucker? If so, I will fuck that up as well.

Hunter kills the engine. His dad likes to buy him flashy presents, like this Audi for Hunter's sixteenth. I gotta give it to him, though. It's a smooth ride.

"Just one thing," Hunter says. "Asher Rossi and Walker Murphy are here."

I clench my teeth and growl deep. Those fuckers let this happen to her. Why are they here? I want to kill them just as much as the fucker who drugged her. They should have taken care of her, not let her get drugged.

"They're just as angry, okay? Asher is gonna be Mila's stepbrother, man. We talked; he wants to kill the guy too. But we said we would all do it together, for Mila. We've been waiting on you, but you didn't answer your phone."

I nod.

"I didn't know you were working today?"

I normally tell them when I'm working. They like to

know where I am…or, more specifically, where I'm not. Like at The Shed, fighting.

I don't answer him, and he lets out a sigh but shakes his head. "We have him in there, but we're gonna let you throw the first punch, okay?"

Hunter knows I need that; I need to be the first and last to inflict pain. They can have their fun too. But I need it like I need air.

Hunter hasn't mentioned what happened back at Jace's earlier. I'm glad because I don't have an answer.

We make our way around the back. There is scrap metal laying around, and shards of broken glass crunch under my boots. When we round the corner, I hear voices. We walk through a door that's been busted off its hinges; it lays at an odd angle, covered in graffiti. Littered inside are beer bottles, rubbish, and a dead rat. It smells just as shit as it looks.

I kick one of the bottles and it skitters along the ground, hitting stones, and the sound echoes within the large, open warehouse.

Sunlight filters through broken windows, and I see the four of them, standing there. They surround a guy with bleached hair who is tied to a chair in the middle of the room.

"Just in time, the party can start now," Jace greets me.

I crack my knuckles and my neck. This is my type of party.

The guy, some skinny fucker in chinos, starts shaking his head at me like I'm here to listen and save him. "I didn't touch her, man, I swear. It wasn't me. I don't need to drug girls to get them into bed."

I look over to Asher and Walker. I've never spoken to them before, but I trust their judgment on this. It happened under their watch, and Mila means something to the King's wide receiver. They shake their heads, telling me all I need to know.

"Tony, you're a fucking piece of shit scumbag," Asher spits at him. "Bryce has cameras all over his place. We all sat down and watched them, and guess what we saw?"

"Please." the piss ant cries out. '

"It was you and your bleached-blond head as you dropped a pill into her cup while she danced."

I feel my tooth crack. They had cameras and caught him doing this. I growl, it's deep and throaty and the fucker starts to shake.

"You weren't even invited to the party. You snuck in like a fucking sly prick. Do you even know who she is?" Asher is pacing now, his hands balled into fists.

I might not like the guy, but I can trust he is gonna see this through today. He will make sure for Mila's sake, and for the sake of other girls, that this fucker pays for what he did.

"She's just some trashy bitch," the fucker screams out at Asher.

All eyes turn to him now, and I love the expression on his face as he realizes he just said the wrong thing. To five very angry football players.

I take a step forward. It's slow and calculated. I want him pissing his pants before he leaves here. Normally, I wouldn't hit someone that couldn't fight back. But when my fist collides with his nose, I hear the crunch of it breaking. His head snaps back and I step back and grin. He lets out a cry that reverberates around the warehouse. Blood is running down each nostril, and I take a sick kind of pleasure from watching it.

"The fuck is wrong with you? You can't just tie me up

and beat me," he screams back at me, as if I'm the crazy one.

He's the one who thought it was okay to drug a girl and rape her. Breaking his nose is only a small step toward letting him know how crazy I really am.

He spits blood on the floor at my feet, and I look down at it and I growl again. "She isn't some trashy bitch. If I ever find out you've done this again, I will come for you. Only, next time, you won't be breathing."

I nod to Jace to untie him. It's not a fair fight, five against one, even without his hands tied behind his back. But it's more fun if he thinks he has a chance against us. Even if the other four didn't fight him, I would lay waste to him in less than a minute.

It surprises me that Asher is the first to move in on him as the fucker stands up.

"She's my stepsister." He grabs Tony by the shoulders and brings his knee up to the guy's guts. The fucker groans and stumbles as he grips his stomach. But he doesn't get a breather; Jace is next to move toward him.

"She's my girl." His voice is deep, and warning. He brings back his left fist, but the fucker sees it and flinches, turning his face. Jace lets his arm swing and smashes it right into the fucker's ear, who lets out a piercing scream.

Jace is right-handed, so the blow isn't as strong as it would be with his right, but he's gotta protect his throwing arm. If the fucker thought that hurt, he still has me to deal with last. He'll know what real pain is soon.

Hunter doesn't give the fucker a chance to right himself. He sweeps his foot out low and takes Tony's feet out from under him. He lands on his arm with a sickening crunch and groans. Hunter kicks him in the side repeatedly. When he finally stops, he bends over the fucker. "And she's mine," Hunter spits down at him.

The fucker rolls away and slowly tries to scramble for his feet. But Walker is there, his knee connecting with Tony's face as he flies back. "She's my friend."

The blood runs down the fucker's nose. His brow and lip are split, but it's not enough. He needs to learn his lesson, and I'm the one to give it to him. I grab him by his hair and yank him up so he can see my face—the last thing he's gonna remember when I leave here.

"She's mine," I growl, before my steel-toe boot connects with his limp dick. I let go of his hair, and he drops back to the floor with a strangled cry that has the other four flinching and cupping their jewels. His once-tan chinos are now shades of brown and red. He doesn't move; he just sobs on the dirty warehouse floor.

I turn and walk out, my vision swimming with all the things he could have done to her. I need air and to leave before I kill him.

I'd said she was mine.

"Fuck," I cry out as I smash my fist into the metal wall.

Mila can never be mine.

TWENTY-TWO
MILA

As soon as Roman stormed out after kissing me, Asher called. He was freaked out that I'd left the car behind and he hadn't been able to find me. Jace had taken the phone from me, and after some yelling and growling, he calmed down and stalked into his room, with my phone, slamming the door to talk to Asher in private.

I'd started to remember what had happened the night before, and it made me sick to my stomach that I hadn't been as careful as I thought. How could I have let my guard down like that? I was almost...raped.

I'd thought I was playing it safe by not drinking. But even completely sober...*fuck*. I'm so stupid. It can happen anytime. You don't have to be intoxicated to not notice someone slipping something into your drink. You can be sober, dancing and having a good time.

It hadn't taken long for Asher to turn up at Jace's with Walker in tow. As soon as Asher saw me, he hugged me tight to his chest. He told me how sorry he was and that he would take care of me. I hadn't wanted to talk about it. I was already emotional and confused after a long night and even stranger morning. Mostly, I was grateful nothing worse had happened and those girls clued into what was going on.

Asher gave me my bag, told me that my Dad thought I came home last night, and to lock the doors behind me. I fished my keys out and did just that. I locked the doors, ran upstairs, and took a long, scalding shower.

Knocking at the door woke me from a nap. I was worried who it would be. I wasn't ready to face the three of *them* after what happened that morning. But Grady's face appeared with a huge smile, a bag of popcorn, and chocolates, so I let him in.

"Let's watch movies...like old times."

My smile faltered only slightly. I was glad to not be alone with my thoughts, and Grady was safe. I could trust him not to kiss me or make me talk about what had happened with his brother, or more so, with Roman. Because he'd seen that...hell, he saw me in my underwear, too.

But he acted as if it didn't happen, and I silently thanked him for that.

The movies we use to watch were fairy tales. The movie Grady chose was a different type of fairy tale. There were hot scenes that made me flush with heat, making me acutely aware that Grady sat right beside me. I could hear him breathing deeply, and he shifted slightly, grazing my hand with his. My heart sped up, and I didn't know it if was good that it was Grady here...or if things just got more complicated.

That had been Saturday. Grady left, and I spent my Sunday overanalyzing everything that had happened with Jace and Roman and the weird tension with Grady.

Monday comes faster than I would have liked, and I still haven't spoken to any of the guys. I'm not sure if they're mad at me. Are they talking to me now? Or are they only jerking off and kissing me?

I hate not knowing. It makes my stomach all twisted up.

I don't know what to expect when I get into Grady's car and he drives me to school. Did he feel the weird tension between us Saturday? Or am I imagining things? I'm more nervous now than I was when I started at a new school in a whole other state.

I need my own car. I will have to ask Dad if I can get one. Just something cheap to run around in. Hell, if I have to ask Mom, I will. That's how nervous I am about seeing Grady. I'm willing to call my mom to avoid him.

I hold onto the brass doorknob and release a deep breath. I have this. I'm strong. I'll walk out there with confidence and get this over with.

The sun hits my face as soon as I step outside, and I smile at the beautiful day. Nothing like sunshine to make you feel cheerful. I put my hand up to block the glare of the sun and look over to where Grady parks his car.

It's not there.

My stomach drops. He left me.

I walk to the curb and look down the street to see if he might have parked somewhere else. But I know that's not the case. I'm stalling, trying to figure out what to do. It's too late to call Sadie and Cadence. It would make them late if they have to come get me now.

I glance at my phone. I have Grady's number. Maybe I should text him? Ask him if he forgot about me? I turn back to my house and contemplate taking the day off. Dad will be okay if I say I'm sick. He'll believe me.

"Hey, Mila."

I spin and see Jace coming toward me. His eyes are squinting from the glare, but he looks happy to see me. He stops at his car, the black SUV, and opens the back door to throw his bag in.

"Hey, ah, have you seen Grady this morning?" I ask.

Seeing Jace for the first time since that…well, the whole jerking off thing has made me very aware of what he's hiding under those shorts of his. Fuck, will I be this worked up around him from now on? Now that we've crossed some strange boundary in our friendship?

If that's what this is—a friendship? He didn't like me last week…now, I have no idea.

Jace's smile is a slow, sly one as his eyes roam up and down my body. I'm very aware of the pink dress I chose to wear today with my white Converse. My pulse picks up under his gaze, and I lick my lips.

He leans against the slick, black metal and nods. "Yeah, Makai called, said he was having car trouble. I told Grady I'll give you a lift today so he can help his friend."

Huh, okay. That sounds like a good reason. Unless Grady is avoiding me and lied about his friend's car trouble. Ugh, I need to stop overthinking this shit. Nothing happened. It's all in my head.

"Okay."

I round Jace's car to the passenger side. When I open the door, he's chucking clothes and empty water bottles into the back seat, and I raise my brow at him. Jace is a slob. And I thought his room was a mess. This takes the cake.

"You need to clean your car."

He gives a deep, throaty chuckle. "Been meaning to.

Don't normally have anyone else in here but Roman, so I'm kinda lazy about it."

I smile at that as I climb in. As soon as his door closes, the scent of his cologne hits me. It's musky but sweet. Or maybe the musky smell is his car? I hide my smile at that thought.

There's an awkward silence between us as we drive to school. He doesn't speak to me, and I nervously chew my nail as I peer out the window. I don't know if I should bring up what happened in his bedroom. That's what this awkwardness is, right? He's trying to ignore it, and I am too.

Or is he upset about Roman kissing me...me kissing him back? Or because I broke their pact again? He didn't really talk to me after I mentioned that. Asher had called and that was the end of our conversation.

My heart races, and I feel like I'm sweating in his leather seat. The A/C is on, but I can't cool down. I just want him to bring it up before it blows up in my face today. I need to know what's going on with us. But he just blares his tunes, tapping on the steering wheel to the beat like this is a normal day. Even if I wanted to talk, he wouldn't hear me over the music.

In the school parking lot, he cuts the engine but doesn't move to get out, so I stay where I am. Is he going to mention it now? Why am I being so silly? I should just ask him. I swallow the lump in my throat. The more I think about it, I realize I don't want to hear him say that nothing's changed. That we aren't friends still.

I look down at my palm, the scar there matching one on Jace's hand. I run my finger over the raised skin.

Jace clears his throat, and I freeze, waiting for the rejection. "Do you remember that day?"

I turn toward him. He holds out his right hand, palm up, showing me his matching scar. That wasn't what I'd been expecting him to say. But I smile as the tension inside me eases slightly.

"How can I forget? You passed out from the sight of blood."

Jace chuckles with a huge grin, and my chest swells at the sound. This is what I wanted when I came back here. This smiling and happy Jace, talking about the good times.

"I'll have you know, I'm okay with blood now. No getting weak in the knees if someone cuts themselves."

"I'm glad you're not fainting at the sight of blood anymore." I reach over and lightly trace his scar with my finger. It's just like mine. I'll never forget that day. It's burned into my memory.

"**M**om *is taking me away. I hate her. I do. I really hate her, Jace.*"

His mom, Ella, is making us sandwiches for lunch. We've been playing football in the backyard for ages, and we're going over to Hunter's house later. It's going to be our last time all together. I'm leaving tomorrow on a plane to move away from everyone who means the world to me.

"It will be okay, Mila." Ella rubs my back as she places the jelly sandwich in front of me. I don't like peanut butter. "You can still talk all the time. You have a phone now, and we got one for Jace, so he can call you every day. We will miss you, but we'll all be together again soon. I promise."

I don't know how she can promise that. Mom made the rule that I can't come back to see Dad. I have to live with her forever. Well, until I'm eighteen. Then, I will run back here. But that's six years away. That's forever.

"I hate your mom, too, Mila. I wish she would just leave you here. I will take care of you," Grady says from the other side of the table. His big chocolate eyes look sad.

"Grady Montero, we don't say we hate people at the dinner table." Ella tsked at him.

"But it's true. I hate her. I don't want you to leave, Mila."

I'm surprised. Grady hasn't spoken to me much lately. Not after he said I'm like an annoying sister he doesn't want. He wants me to stay?

A tear slips from my eye, and I wipe it away. I've been doing nothing but crying the last few days. I don't have enough time to say goodbyes. It's not fair.

"Come on, you two. Eat up, and I will drive you both over to Hunter's. I'm picking Roman up on the way, and I don't want to be late. I told him I would be there at one."

I look up at the large clock on the wall. We have ten minutes to get Roman. I don't know how long it takes to get to his house, but he worries if we're late to get him. He'll get all moody and worked up if we're even a minute late, and Ella knows this too.

I get to spend today with my best friends, my boys, and tomorrow with my dad. He's letting me have this one last day with them, swimming in Hunter's pool and having a fun time before I have to say goodbye.

We've only been swimming for a little while when Hunter's mom says she needs a nap. She leaves us with homemade lemonade and a plate full of Oreos.

Hunter's shoulders fall at the mention of her taking a nap. I'd seen enough to know that she likes to drink until she falls asleep, and that's what she means by taking a nap. I quickly hug Hunter close to me, and he tenses up a little before he gingerly wraps his arms around my back. But he stands funny, with his legs far away from me.

"Are you okay?" I ask.

He nods against my shoulder. "Yeah, I just have a sore back."

Before I can speak, he turns and runs, jumping into the deep end of the pool. I'd been asking about his mom, but now I'm worried he's hurt his back. Did I tackle him too hard earlier when we were pretending to be MMA fighters? The guys know I like to use my full strength when we fight, but maybe I was too rough.

Warm arms wrap around my waist from behind and hug me to a warm, bare chest. Roman. I smile to myself. I love when he hugs me like this. It isn't a friend hug. It's what I've seen couples do, and it gives me butterflies every time.

"I have an idea," he whispers in my ear.

I spin to look at him over my shoulder, and the gleam in his eyes has me nodding. This is gonna be something good. He holds my hand and calls out to Jace and Hunter to follow us. But not before he grabs his backpack.

We go down to the secret part on Hunter's property that's surrounded by trees. There are two chairs and a broken pool lounge that we sit on, but out here is where we do our secret things. Like when Jace lit firecrackers he stole from his dad. Or Hunter stole the big sugar bowl from his kitchen, and we ate it with our hands until our tummies hurt.

We wanted a treehouse here, but Hunter's dad said no. That we aren't babies anymore. You don't have to be a baby to have a treehouse. It's for everyone to have fun. We didn't like Hunter's dad after that. Maybe that's why Hunter's mom always drinks and sleeps. So she doesn't have to listen to him being mean.

Roman dumps his bag into the dirt and turns to look at the three of us who stand around him, waiting to see why he brought *us out here. I'm hoping he has fireworks, but I'll keep that thought to myself.*

"I want us to make a blood pact." *Roman smiles wildly.*

I...what? I look at Jace and Hunter, then back to Roman who is nodding at me.

"What?" *Hunter asks, and Roman's brows furrow like he doesn't understand the question.*

"What's a blood pact?" *I ask as Roman pulls out a pock-etknife from his bag.*

Jace takes a step back and shakes his head. "No, you're not gonna cut me with that." *He holds his hands up, and he looks scared.*

Why would Roman cut him? Oh...that's how he gets the blood.

Roman flicks it out, and the silver of the blade shines in the filtered sunlight coming through the tree canopy above. "It's sharp, I made sure," *he says as he turns it over in his hand.*

Where the hell did Roman get that? Did he steal it from his dad, or is it his?

Roman looks over to me and smiles as he shows me the blade. I lean in and touch it.

"A blood pact is when you cut your hand and the other person does too. And you press the cuts together. You make a pact in blood. It's for life. I want us to be best friends for life," *Roman explains to me and Hunter. Jace must already know what it is.*

I glance at Jace, and he keeps shaking his head.

I look down at my hand. Roman wants to cut me? That will hurt, wont it? It won't hurt more than me leaving, though. And I don't want to lose my best friends. I want them for life. If this pact makes it for life, then I want that.

I step forward and hold out my hand to Roman.

"Mila, no. Don't. It's gonna hurt."

I turn back to a very scared Jace and frown. "Not as much as losing you forever. I want us to be best friends for life."

Roman grunts and I see blood dripping from the palm of his right hand. He's left-handed. I don't think about that until now. The rest of us are right-handed. I look down at my own hands as he takes my right one in his. His blood is warm and slippery on mine, but I don't care. He is my best friend; I will love him forever.

"Are you sure?" he whispers, and I realize I'm clenching my teeth as my whole body stands tense. I peer into his blue eyes. I can see the love he has for me there. He wants this...needs this as much as me.

I nod. "Just do it fast?"

I close my eyes as I feel the metal slice into my skin, and the pain is like a flash of heat, over within a second. Red starts to pour out from around where he sliced. It's shallow, not deep. But it will leave a scar. I feel Hunter brush my shoulder as he stands beside me.

"Best friends for life." He looks at me as he holds his right palm out to Roman.

I watch this time, looking down at his hand. Roman's knife is sharp. It slices through Hunter's skin with ease. It's a strange sight, seeing someone cut another. Roman is so good at this, it worries me he has done it before. Not a blood pact...but cut something.

Once Hunter's hand is done, we all turn to Jace, whose face is pale. He holds his hand over his mouth like he's about to be sick.

"Are you okay, Jace?" I'm worried he's going to fall over. He doesn't look well.

"Does blood make you queasy?" Roman asks, cocking his head to the side as he tries to read Jace. Roman approaches, and

Jace's eyes widen at the blood dripping down Roman's wrist now, then to the knife in his left hand.

"No," Jace replies, but it comes out soft, like a whisper, as his knees waver.

Holy crap, Jace doesn't like the sight of blood. I grow concerned that if he doesn't join the blood pact, he won't be best friends for life with us, and I would hate that. He needs to do it.

"Just look away," I tell him. I didn't look, and it doesn't hurt. It just stings a little.

"No, no, I can't. Please, I think I'm gonna be sick."

Roman stops and watches Jace. He doesn't say anything; he just waits and watches him. He lets Jace catch his breath.

We are all silent as the color returns to Jace's face. He closes his eyes and holds out his right palm to Roman. His knees tremble, and I feel sick. He doesn't want to do it. I don't want him to do it if he doesn't want to. He can still be part of the blood pact without cutting. We will make sure.

"Do it, quick, before I change my mind."

And with the swift slice of the blade, Roman cuts the palm of Jace's hand, and Jace lets out a small, painful cry that stabs me right in my heart. A tear rolls down my cheek as my best friend holds his hand to his chest and lets out a strangled sob. He is the smallest of us all, and I sometimes forget that.

We all crowd around Jace and press our cuts to each other's. I press mine into Jace's while Roman and Hunter do the same. Then we switch until we all have shared blood. Jace doesn't open his eyes at all while we do this. I ignore the tears rolling down his face for now. I will hug him and fix his hand up when we are done.

"Blood friends for life," Roman cheers, and I smile up at him and repeat it. The other two do too, but I can't keep my eyes from Roman. This is more than friendship. This is family. We are a family.

I hear a loud gasp, and I break my gaze from Roman to see Jace. He's looking down at our hands. The bleeding has slowed, but there's a lot of blood. Jace's eyes land on mine, and his face turns to ash as his eyes roll into his head. My heart stops.

"Jace," we all call out as we try to catch him before he drops to the ground.

The memory makes my chest heavy. Our lives were perfect before I left and fucked everything up. I look into Jace's eyes, not expecting to see the same sadness I feel inside.

"Blood friends for life," Jace says.

TWENTY-THREE
HUNTER

Mila steps out from Jace's car—what the fuck? She smiles as she swings her bag over her shoulder, and he comes up to stand close beside her. They're talking. They laugh, and I feel like I've been lied to. Deceived by the person I've called my best friend for ten years.

I spent yesterday with my dad and mom. They argued and fought like always. But yesterday, I spoke up. I told them to get a divorce already. I hate this shit between them; they aren't happy, and neither am I. Mom cried, and Dad said I made her miserable, that it was my fault she was upset. He then left, saying he won't be back until sometime next month, and he won't be at my game on Friday.

He never wants to attend my games. I'm surprised he bothered to show at last Friday's game. He told me how disappointed he was in my efforts, that I wasn't a great football player, so I should stop wasting my time. That I need to focus on academics and not sports. Sports get you nowhere.

He doesn't care that I enjoy it. That's what I love about football. A little girl with pale blonde hair and a huge smile introduced me to a game that I fell in love with. I'm good at it, too, no matter what he says. I had scouts checking me out during sophomore year. I could get a scholarship and play for a college team. But Dad won't allow that. *"No son of mine is playing football in college."*

I don't know what his problem is. Every chance he gets, he punishes me for loving football. And for being good at it.

I sit in my car, staring at where Jace and Mila had been. I can't stop thinking of how Jace lied to me. He wants her for himself, and he's done everything he can to keep me from her.

There's a bang on my window, and I startle, not expecting it. *Roman.* I rest my head back and close my eyes. Not that he cares. He bangs his fist on the window again.

I'm in a funk and don't want to see Mila and Jace right now. This morning, I'd been excited to see her. I was gonna ask her if she wanted to come over to my place later, after training. But now…her and Jace. I'm not ready for that.

It's bullshit, the way Jace went on about the pact and how it still stands or she will break our friendships. Well, he has just gone and done that. He fucked me over, lied to me about Mila being with Asher Rossi, and without even blinking, he takes her from us. Roman deserves a fair chance at her too. After that kiss… How can I compete with a kiss like that?

I get out and Roman takes a step back. His knuckles are all cut up and there's a bruise on his cheek. Shit, I didn't know he was fighting. Did Jace? I hadn't spoken to either of them yesterday. I was busy taking care of Mom after Dad left.

"You fought last night?"

He shrugs, like it doesn't matter.

It does. I hate that shit. I hate all of it, but I don't want him to lie. I'm still waiting on him to tell me about The Sons of Death MC, but I don't see him doing that anytime soon. He's keeping more secrets than I like, and I can't protect him if he does that.

"We alright?" he asks as he waits for me.

I grab my bag and slam the door of my car a little too hard. "Just peachy."

I start toward the front door of the school, but I turn when I see Roman still standing there. His eyes are on his feet, and I realize what he had asked me. "We alright," not "are you alright."

Fuck. I rake my hand through my short hair and let out a deep sigh. I'm not upset with Roman. I can't take this shit with Jace out on him.

Hell, to be honest, that kiss he had with Mila—it was hot as fuck. But I wouldn't tell him that. Never seen him kiss a girl before, but if they're all like that, I can understand why so many of the girls at school want him.

I stride over to where he's standing, my hand reaching out to his shoulder. I clasp it, and I feel him tense under the contact. I know he hates being touched, but I want to comfort him. He needs to listen to me.

"Sorry, I was fucked up in my own head. I didn't hear you right. We're alright, man. I'm not upset with you. Okay?"

He shrugs again. I don't think he'll believe anything I say right now. But he needs to know.

"You kissed her. And, I get it, she's your dream girl.

Hell, she's my dream girl too. But I'm not mad at you for doing it. I would have done the same thing."

He looks over at me and I nod. But, really, we know I wouldn't have done that. I wouldn't press her against a door and wrap my hand around her throat and steal a kiss. A kiss she chased after.

No, I was the dumbass standing there, staring at her body, my cock hard as a rock as her breasts strained against the fabric of her lace bra. I wanted to see the color of her nipples. I wanted to kiss and suck on them until they were hard nubs. But I didn't move; I just stared.

"I don't know what to do," he mutters.

I take a step back to read his face. What does he mean? "With Mila?"

He nods.

"Well, I just saw her smiling and happy with Jace, so if you want her, you're gonna have to fight for her. Cause the asshole isn't playing fair right now."

Roman shakes his head and lets out a deep sigh. "I don't want...her," is all he says as he storms off toward the school entrance.

I stand there, dumbfounded. He doesn't want Mila? Then what the hell was that intense kiss all about?

don't have many classes with the guys, so I don't see either of them until history. Even then, it's not the one I want to talk to. I need to talk to Jace, but he has World History...with Mila.

Roman sits beside me. He pretends to listen to the teacher in here. He's never been great at school, and the teachers don't help. They see him as a dumb football player from the wrong side of the tracks who doesn't want to learn. What they don't know is that I taught him how to read and write. The school system let him down, and at the age of seven, I taught him something they were supposed to.

Just like he's staring at the teacher as she drones on, I'm doing the same today. I pull my phone out—it's hidden under the desk—and send Jace a text.

Hunter: We need to talk.

It doesn't take long for him to reply.

Jace: I know.

I lean back in my chair, my eyes roaming around the room. When they catch on Britney, she smiles and waves. I hate the girl, I truly do. What Jace sees in her, I haven't a clue. She's clingy as fuck, and *oh fuck*...she's with Jace. They're still together. She probably has no idea what went down Saturday between Jace and Mila.

Hell, I don't fully know what went down. Jace wouldn't talk about it. But he had that look. I knew that look...I used to wear it a lot. Until Mila came back. Now the only person I want to put that look on my face is her.

Jace: Meet me at lunch.

TWENTY-FOUR
MILA

Today has been so weird, and I still don't know where I stand with the guys.

I told Jace I didn't want to sit at his table, but he insisted. Then Emerson overheard and wanted me to sit with him too, so I agreed. Jace told Em what he thought about that idea, but I just rolled my eyes. Jace needs to get over himself. I can be friends with Emerson if I want.

I've been hoping to speak to the three of them together, but Roman isn't here. Hunter strolls over to the table, and the look on his face is hard to read.

Then Britney fucking Montlake appears out of nowhere, and from the look on her face, she's not thrilled to see me here. Far from it. I don't think she likes me sitting at their table.

"Hey, Britney. *Shit*," Jace says, appearing caught. "We need to talk about us."

"What the fuck?" Britney gives off an ear-piercing screech.

My mouth drops. Holy fuck. They're still together? Shit, how could I have forgotten. And after what we did on Saturday...I feel so guilty. I might hate her, but hell, I don't want to be the chick he cheats on his girlfriend with. It's cheating, yeah? He didn't touch me... No, I touched him. I feel my cheeks heat at the memory.

"What the fuck, Jace? You're fucking her now? After everything you said to me?"

I grit my teeth and tense at her words. Fuck this shit. I'm out of here. I get up and push away from the table.

Jace and Hunter call out to me, but I don't look back. I continue to leave the cafeteria and walk into the warm sunshine of the day. I take a deep breath and shake my head and body.

I shouldn't have sat next to Jace. He hasn't spoken to me about what happened. I don't know if we're friends. He's acting like we are but never said anything. I rub the scar on my palm and think about how things have changed so fast from the moment we got to school. Only last week not one of the guys would look at me, and now they want me to sit with them. Chat and laugh. It's surreal.

All I want is my three best friends back. But Saturday changed things in a way I hadn't been expecting.

I spot Roman sitting under a tree. He's hunched over and picking at grass shards. Hell, even Roman wouldn't speak to me earlier in class. He wouldn't even look at me.

I want what we had, before I left. I don't want to go back to what we were last week, but I know the kiss I shared with Roman is why he's avoiding me.

I don't say anything as I sit on the grass beside him. His hair has fallen like a curtain around his face, but he tenses up. He knows I'm here.

"I need to talk to you," I start, but he doesn't look at me. He doesn't even speak. "Roman?"

He grunts and picks more of the grass. I think that's the best I'm getting out of him for an acknowledgement.

"I don't want things to be weird, you know, after…"

Fuck, now I can't even say what happened. Because that wasn't just a kiss, and I don't want him to think it didn't mean something to me. No, it was an earth-shattering kiss, and as much as I want to do it again, I can sense he doesn't want to talk to me after it. And it will mess up everything I want if we do kiss. I want my friends back. I want Roman back in my life, picking flowers and hugs every day.

"Can we be friends again? Like we used to?"

He's quiet for a moment, and I watch the other students as they pass us by. Some look at us, and girls giggle as the pass by, checking Roman out. I can't blame them; he grew up to be so good-looking. Not that he wasn't always. I had a crush on him for a long time, but the same goes for the other two.

Still, the pact is important. It's what's going to keep them together. I can't ever pick one of them; I wouldn't do that. The pact is the best thing they ever came up with, and I can't mess this up again. I need them all back in my life.

I notice that Roman's knuckles have split open, and blood trickles down his fingers. What the hell happened to cause that?

"Shit, Roman. Your hand is bleeding."

He sits up and looks at me, really looks at me. I swear, for a moment, I can see something lurking in the depths of his eyes. Something dark that's been there the whole time. Only, it's closer to the surface now, and it scares me.

He needs me more than I need him. He's broken, he's hurt, and the only one to blame is me for not being there for him when he needed me.

"God, Roman, I'm so fucking sorry." I choke back tears. "I'm sorry I left you all alone. I didn't want to, please believe me when I say that. I was a sad little girl who couldn't bear hearing about how her friends were all having fun without her, so she locked herself away and cried. Until she was only a fragment of the little girl her friends once knew.

"When the girl emerged, she'd turned into a broken puppet with vacant eyes, dancing for her mom and putting on a show. She used vices just to get through the week. Alcohol, drugs...*sex*. Until she got on that plane and knew she was coming back to her best friends. That she could finally live again. Be happy and free."

I reach for his right hand, and he lets me touch him. I flip it over and see the scar there. I trace it with my thumb. His skin is rough, but the scar is still raised like mine. "Blood friends for life."

He doesn't say anything, but he doesn't stop me from touching his hand either. We sit in silence until his fingers move to hold my hand. My chest swells with hope.

"Friends, Mila. I want us to be friends. Nothing more."

He doesn't say anything else, and I don't either. I understand what he's saying. He gave me the best kiss of my life, and I will never get to experience it again. But, in return, I have his friendship, and that's what I wanted to begin with.

As soon as the bell rings for class, I reluctantly let go of Roman's hand and head to my locker. I'm grabbing my books when I see Roman, Jace, and

Hunter walking out of the school. They have classes, but they're leaving?

I follow them. I want to see what they're up to, and I find them close to where Jace parked his car.

"Fuck you, the pact is total bullshit, and now you fucked up my chance to be with her." Hunter shoves Jace, and I gasp.

Holy shit, they're fighting over me.

Roman holds Hunter back as Jace puffs up his chest. "What happened between us...fuck, I want it to happen again, okay? You want me to say sorry? Well, I'm not. Just like Roman kissed her. He isn't sorry."

Roman shoves Jace then, and he stumbles back. Roman doesn't say anything, and Jace continues to stand his ground.

Fuck, I can't have them fighting. They're best friends. Hell, they have a football game on Friday, and they can't be fighting. They work together so amazingly on the field, and I don't want to be the reason we lose another game. Not that I totally blame myself for that last one.

I need to talk to Jace and Hunter. Roman has already made himself clear, and I'm glad. Just like with Asher, we need to set some boundaries. When Jace swings at Hunter, I scream. Jace misses and stumbles.

"Stop, stop fighting." I run at them. They all spin on their heel to watch me running, and I stop once I'm between Jace and Hunter.

"Just stop, okay? Nothing is gonna happen." I look up to Jace. "Friendship is more important than what we did, okay?" I spin around to make sure they're all listening. "No kissing or touching and no sex. Friends."

There is a loaded pause in the air. I feel the tension

crackling between them, and I look to Jace, thinking he's about to explode. But it's not him.

"You touched her?" Hunter growls out, as if that's the only thing he heard.

I throw my hands up. Maybe we can't be friends; maybe the whole sex thing is an issue. People used to tell me that I couldn't be friends with boys. Males and females just can't; they'll always want more. I told them it wasn't true. That we could all stay friends. Even though I went through periods of crushes on the boys, that's all they were. I got over them, and we stayed friends.

"No, I didn't touch her," Jace replies.

That seems to calm Hunter down a little. I let out a sigh. How did I think this would ever work? Can I start today over again?

"She touched me."

My mouth drops open, and I turn in time to see Hunter lunge for Jace. I step out of the way as Hunter gets Jace into a headlock.

"Fuck, stop it." Roman grabs the back of Hunter's shirt, and it rips while Roman tries to pry him off Jace.

Jace slams his fist into Hunter's gut, repeatedly, and the two of them wrestle and grunt. I have no idea what to do. When they used to fight, it was easier. I could break it up. But now I'm almost a foot shorter than them; it's a little hard to jump in and stop them.

"Jace, Hunter, stop!" Grady calls out as he runs to us.

He helps Roman pull them apart. Hunter's face is flushed, and he coughs before trying to fix his tee. But it's too far gone.

Jace shakes himself off and bounces on his feet, ready for another round.

"I was told there are three Rebels out here, fighting. Over a girl. Guess what?" Grady asks.

No one answers. Hunter and Jace just glare daggers at each other and ignore Grady.

"I knew it was you they were talking about the minute I heard it." Grady lets out a loud sigh as he throws his hands up. "Go to class, and we can talk about this after training."

All three of them look at Grady and nod. Roman is the first to leave. Hunter follows behind him, and Jace looks to me before cursing and walking to his car.

I move to call out to him, but Grady wraps his arm around my shoulder. "Leave him. He's upset with what happened between him and Hunter. If you want, I can drive you home? I have study hall right now, but I can drive you home and come back in time for training."

I nod. That would be for the best. I can feel the eyes of students watching me, and I just need to go home. I feel exposed in a way I hadn't been expecting to experience today, and it's too much.

I've made everything worse by returning here and thinking I can start up my friendships from four years ago like nothing has changed.

Everything has changed.

TWENTY-FIVE
MILA

"Would it give you comfort to know I've been waiting for this since you returned?"

I turn to Grady. Is he serious? He expected *that* to happen?

"No." My voice is higher than usual.

He just chuckles. "Really? What did you think would happen when the same old sassy Mila, with a hot body, returned to three sixteen-year-old guys who only think with their dicks? Of course, they're going to fight over you. They had to make a pact at the age of ten to stop fighting over you, and that was before you got all…" He waves his hand at me. "Sexy."

Well, now that he put it that way…*fuck.*

To be honest, I didn't have much time to think about it when I was on the plane. I didn't think about how much I had changed…or they had. Instead, I remembered all the good times.

I smirk at Grady. "You think I have a hot body and I'm sexy?"

He groans and shakes his head, but I can see the smile on his face. "You're just as bad as them, Mimi."

I laugh. "You know, you're pretty wise for someone who is only a year older. Where do you get all your wisdom from, oh wise one?" I prop my hand under my chin and gaze up at him from the middle console, a playful smile on my face as I bat my lashes.

He looks down at me and snorts. "I hang around smart people. You should try it."

I laugh again. "You know...I used to have a big crush on you." I sit back and watch his expression. I'd never told him, or anyone, about my crushes. But, for some reason, I want him to know now.

"Really? I had one on you too."

I blink and gape at him. *What?* He had a crush on me? When? How?

"Why didn't you say something?"

He shrugs and glances at me briefly before looking back to the road. "What, like I would've ever had a chance. You had three best friends who'd been in love with you since the day they met you. I knew I couldn't compete with that, and that's okay. A childhood crush is just that— a crush."

"You might have had a chance?" I say, though it comes out as a question.

He shakes his head. "Hell, Mimi. You gave them all their first kiss. You never came to see me that day. You never asked me for your first kiss."

I toy with the strap of my bag as I watch the houses go past, thinking about what he'd said. I didn't go to him. But that's because I thought he didn't like me. Or had I known, deep down, that he wasn't for me?

"You told me I was like an annoying little sister you

never wanted. You made me think I was like a sister to you. I cried for three days, Grady. My dad didn't know what was wrong with me and wanted me to see a doctor. But I was just heartbroken that the boy I had a crush on for a whole year thought of me as a sister...an annoying one, at that."

Neither of us speak for the rest of the drive. He pulls into my driveway, and I unbuckle myself. I don't look at him. "Thank you, for the lift," I whisper.

"Stop, Mila. Look at me, please."

I glance over under my lashes to see Grady has taken his seat belt off and moved closer to me. My eyes widen at the sudden change, and the air in the car seems thicker somehow. Or maybe my throat is thick with emotion.

"Mila, I told you that because I didn't want my heart broken. I thought if I told you that you're like an annoying sister that you would stay away from me. Hate me. Because if you hated me, there was no way you would find out I was actually in love with you. I was scared you would laugh at me, and that was a worse fear than you hating me."

My heart drops at his admission. I never would have done that to him. But he couldn't have known that.

"Grady..." I reach out and take his hand.

Fuck, today has been a clusterfuck of emotions. I hadn't expected the car ride to go this way when I got in. Or that confessing my crush on him back then would result in Grady admitting that the feelings were mutual.

"I'd just turned thirteen," he says. "My body was changing, and I didn't know what to do with all my feelings or the hormones. I was a stupid teenage boy, with a crush on his younger brother's best friend.

"I'm sorry I made you feel that way. I didn't know. I

thought it was one-sided. That you only saw me as Jace's big brother. That you never thought of me as anything more." He groans. "And when I heard about your first kisses two weeks ago, that cemented it. I was never on your radar, and it reminded me again how I never had a chance."

He leans back into his headrest and closes his eyes, running his other hand down his face. Oh god. That's how I felt when he said I was like a sister.

He surprises me by drawing closer. His hand moves to my face, brushing my hair behind my ear before cupping my cheek. It feels nice, and my stomach flutters at the gesture. Grady's big eyes—the same color as Jace's—roam my face like he's looking at me for the first time. Really looking at me.

I study his face too. He has a sharper jawline now. The stubble on his cheek is dark, and I itch to touch it. To see if it's scratchy or soft. He's grown bigger in the past four years; his chest is wider, and even his hands are huge.

When his eyes land on my lips, I unconsciously wet them. He's always had kissable lips. Is he going to kiss me? Do I want him to? My breathing becomes more rapid as my lips part.

He moves in, pressing his warm lips against mine, and I close my eyes at the touch. I gasp as I arch into him, reaching out to cup his cheek as he deepens the kiss. His stubble is rough, and I rub my thumb over it. He moans, his tongue sweeping over my lower lip, and I open to meet his with mine.

God, he's a good kisser. His scent is intoxicating as I reach down and pull his black tee toward me, like I can't get close enough to him.

His phone rings, and we both pull apart abruptly. I

touch my fingers to my swollen lips. Grady looks ruffled as he gives me a gorgeous grin. He looks down at the caller ID. Jace.

Fuck, I curse myself internally.

I thought the shit that happened before I got into the car was confusing and messy enough, but now…confusing and messy doesn't even begin to describe it.

Grady answers, and before he can say anything to me, I open the door and step out, slamming it behind me.

"Mila," he calls from his open window, but I'm already at the front door, unlocking it. I need to speak to someone. Someone who can help me understand what the fuck I'm doing. Because, clearly, I'm not thinking straight.

"If you're handing out kisses to everyone, why am I missing out again?" Asher rolls over on my bed to my nightstand to grab another chocolate out of my secret sweet drawer.

I round the bed and slam it shut, almost catching his fingers. "Because we established you're gonna be my step-brother, *maybe,* and sex is already off the table. I need help."

He laughs. "You need serious help. A shrink, maybe?"

I smack him with my pillow. He raises his arms, and I hit him again. He's laughing at me as I huff and drop to the floor beside my bed and lean my head against the wall. He rolls over to the edge and looks down at me.

"You know, I had to fake illness to come here. I thought it was a real emergency. I'm supposed to be at training with your dad."

"This is a real emergency."

To be honest, I didn't think about that when I called him. I told him I needed him and I'm at home. He was fast. I guess, after what happened at the party the other night, he's worried about me. I have no idea why I called him. He was the first person I could think of that could help me.

He sits up and swings his legs off the bed before sitting beside me, his shoulder nudging mine. "So, you kissed Grady Montero? I hope he kisses better than he tackles." I smile and shove him. "Makes sense why he was gunning for me so hard, though."

I look at him, and he shrugs. "He likes you. He probably thought we were a thing as well, so he took it out on me. Jealous that I got the girl." His wiggles his brows, and I shake my head.

"Has anyone told you that you're full of yourself?"

"You can be the first, if you want."

I sigh and rest my head against the wall again. Closing my eyes, I try to imagine what tomorrow will look like. Roman is safe...he wants to just be friends. But do I just want to be friends? Do I truly want to only be friends with any of them after all this time?

I have feelings for each of them. I always have, but I can't pick one over the others. I can't lose any of them again. I want them all, and I know that's being greedy and unrealistic.

"Do you think guys can be friends with girls without sex getting in the way? Or is it always doomed to fail?"

Asher's deep chuckle has me opening my eyes and looking at him. He cocks his head to the side and gives me a warm smile. "Give me your hand."

He holds his hand out, and I arch my brow at him. But I do as he says. He flips my palm facing down, and his hand cups the back of mine as he lowers it to his crotch. I don't pull away as he pushes my palm into his cock, gasping when I feel how hard he is underneath his shorts.

"With you? It's always doomed to fail."

Fuck.

TWENTY-SIX
MILA

"Thank you for coming," I say to Sadie as I quickly close the door to her red coupe. It smells a little funky, but it's better than being in a car with either of my neighbors right now. Funky smell over being trapped in a car with them, any day.

"I want to know what made you call me, and why you're not getting a lift with either of the Montero brothers. Grady and Jace are just so…yummy."

I sag into the soft fabric of the seat and look out the window as we drive past their cars. They won't know I'm not coming with them until I'm already at school.

Closing my eyes, I try to figure out how to answer her. Because, really, it's the truth. They're yummy, and it would make more sense to accept a ride with either of them. Avoiding them won't make the problem go away, but it sure as hell will give me more time to think.

"It's complicated," I reply as I glance out at the people going about their days without all the problems I have. Hell, I wonder if anyone would even call this a problem. Kissing hot boys, touching them…ugh.

"That's a totally boring answer." Sadie shakes her head and laughs.

"Fuck, everything's complicated. I thought I could come back and be friends with the boys like old times. But it's like we all turn into slaves to our hormones once we become teenagers. The whole sex shit is getting in the way…hell, even my future stepbrother has made it clear that it's impossible for girls to just be friends with guys."

"First off, what the hell? Sex? Spill. Was it with Jace? And two, your stepbrother wants to have sex with you? Gross."

I laugh, ignoring the first part, since I want to avoid the topic of Jace right now.

"He's not my stepbrother, officially. My dad is just dating his mom. But if you saw him, you wouldn't be saying *gross*. He's annoyingly hot and funny."

I pull up a photo on my phone, one that we took together at the first Lakeview party he took me to. He has a goofy-ass grin on his face, and I'm sticking out my tongue to the camera. I show Sadie when she stops at a stop sign, and her mouth drops open.

"Get out of here, that's gonna be your stepbrother?"

I nod. "Well, that's if my dad marries his mom, of course. They've only been dating a few months, I think. It seems serious, though. He's at their place more than he's at home."

"If you don't want him, can I have him?" Sadie winks over at me.

I chuckle and slide the phone back into my bag. "Next Lakeview party I got to, I'll bring you along and introduce you. He's a player, on and off their field. So, just a heads up."

"Oh, one night is good enough for me."

We both laugh.

But I won't be going to any Lakeview parties for a while. Not because of the spiked drink thing—I've boxed that up and put it away on a shelf to be dealt with another time—but more because, after our little chat last night, it would be best to avoid Asher for a few days.

I think the forbidden fruit thing is hanging a little too close now, and it's best to go try some fruit I can actually eat.

But that leaves me wondering what I want. Or rather, who?

I could stay single, I don't need a boyfriend to be happy. But it's nice to have someone to care for and who cares about you in return. Someone who sends a message every morning to say hello, because I'm the first person he wants to speak to when he wakes up. And, at night, I'm the last person he thinks about as he says goodnight.

I sigh. I want that, I do. But I can't have what I want—it's not possible. I need to look outside the boys. My boys. Jace, Hunter, and Roman. I can't have them all, so I won't have one. But I don't want anyone else to have them either.

And what about Grady? *Fuck*. He kissed me, and I kissed him back. I still don't know what that means. Do I want to kiss him again? I don't know. It was a great kiss, but...it's not like when Roman kissed me. Hell, nothing will ever compare to that kiss. Even now, my toes are curling at the thought.

🏈 🏈 🏈

My first class of the day is with Jace and Roman. Only, today, they don't shun me. They don't seem to be fighting anymore, either. Jace smiles when he sees me and pats the desk beside him. Roman sits in front of him and gives me a hint of a smile as I pass him.

"Hey," I say as I sit down, dumping my books on my desk with a thud.

"Did you get a lift with Grady?" Jace questions, and I shake my head.

"No, with Sadie."

He furrows his brow and shrugs. Okay, snob boy. Is the football star too popular to know the rest of the students here?

"I'll have you know, Sadie is nice and funny and actually wanted to be my friend when you were being jerks. So, shame on you, jock boy."

Jace holds his hands up. "Sorry, I don't know everyone. I'm a busy person."

I ignore him and turn to Roman. "Roman?" I ask, and he turns to look at me. He doesn't smile, but he nods in acknowledgment of what I said. "After school today, do you want to come over to work on the assignment together for chem? Or we could work in the library, if that's easier?"

"Got practice till five," he says, and I can't wipe the smile from my face. He's still talking to me. We are all good.

"That's okay. I'll order food, and we can work over dinner. Dad will be happy to see you."

Dad asked me when he's going to start seeing Hunter and Roman over at our place. He said he misses the boys.

I'd pouted, and he just laughed, saying he loves me, but when I left, so did they. He's always looked at them like they're his sons too.

"Okay." Roman nods and turns back to the teacher.

"Do you want to wait around until we finish? I can give you a lift home," Jace offers.

Does he think he's coming over to study with me too?

When I don't answer straightaway, he nods toward the back of Roman. "He has a motorcycle. Just thought, if you need a lift, it might be more comfortable in my car is all."

Oh, wow. I didn't know Roman rode a motorcycle. Fuck, he just went up ten points on the hot scale. I've always wanted to ride one. But I think it would give Dad a heart attack, and he's too young for one of those.

"Yeah, that would be great. As much as I would love to ride with Roman, I think it's best my dad doesn't see me on the back of a motorcycle just yet. I can study in the library while you're training. Who do you play this Friday? It's an away game, right?"

"Yeah, you coming to watch us? We play East Haven Huskies. Mom and Dad will be there. They could give you a lift."

I nod. Yeah, I'll come watch their game. I don't want to miss it. I like this. So far with Jace and Roman, it isn't what I was expecting. But I'm so grateful. It's what I wanted when I came back.

"But you need to wear Rebels colors."

I laugh loudly, and everyone in class turns to me, and the teacher glares daggers. I look down at my desk and shuffle my books, but I can't hide the smile.

Today has started out so perfect. I'm happy. I shouldn't have been so worried.

There's a loud "whoop" in the quiet of the library. There aren't many students here, and I look over to see Hunter, wearing basketball shorts and a red tee, looking at me. His gym bag is slung over his shoulder as he jogs to me.

"Hey, Mila. I got you something to wear for the game on Friday. I packed it in my bag this morning, but I forgot to give it to you earlier." He slams his bag down on the table, and the other student sitting close by stares at him.

I wave my hand at Hunter to lower his voice. "Shhh… have you never been in a library?"

Hunter looks around at everyone gawking at him. He grins and waves at them like he's a royal prince on a tour. *Ugh.* I want to be friends with them again, so I guess I have to deal with Mr. Cocky, popular, football star and the stares from others.

Today, the guys have been nothing but friendly. It was a little jarring at lunch, and I think it might take me a few days to get used to it.

He starts to rummage in his bag, which is full of so much shit. Clothes, shoes, a water bottle, a wet towel…is that half a bag of Doritos?

"It's in here somewhere. I packed it at the bottom, so I wouldn't lose it." He pulls out a bunch of random clothes, and a dirty sock drops onto the table.

I scrunch up my nose at how gross his gym bag is. "God, Hunter, did you pack your whole house in there." Whatever he brought me is probably gonna smell bad if it's at the bottom of all that.

He pauses, a lopsided grin on his face. "Do you know what I pack when I see you?"

Confused I ask, "What do you pack?"

"About eight inches."

My mouth drops open. He didn't. *What the fuck?*

"Hunter," I whisper-yell, shaking my head. I hold my hand over my mouth to stop myself from laughing loudly.

He chuckles like it's the funniest thing ever. He got me good—I walked right into that one.

"God, you're annoying."

He just grins and winks.

Then, he pulls out a red jersey. He proudly shows it to me. It's wrinkled and probably smells like sweaty jock strap, but it just says "Rebels." No number or names. No playing favorites.

I smile, and reaching out, I take it. "Thank you." I hug it to my chest. "This is perfect."

Then the smell hits me, and I dangle it away from myself as I try not to gag. "You might want to wash everything in your bag," I suggest, and he laughs at me as he shoves everything back inside.

"Or burn it," Jace says as he approaches behind Hunter. "You ready to go?" he asks me.

I nod, quickly putting all my books in my bag and holding the jersey. I don't want my books to have this locker-room stink too.

On the way to Jace's car, I start to feel a nervous. Is he going to say something to me in the car about what happened yesterday? With the fight? Did Grady tell him that we kissed?

If he asks, I'll be honest. But if Grady hasn't mentioned it, I won't either. It's not a big deal unless we make it one.

Thankfully, the ride home is normal. Jace sings badly to some tunes on the radio. He tells me how he's been working hard on his passes, and he hopes there will be college scouts coming to his games.

"I know I'm not a top draft pick. I never will be. But I'm good enough for a smaller college. I just need the scholarship. Grady will get one—he's got a four-star rating. He's already gotten offers to a few amazing colleges. I don't want my parents to worry about me."

I understand what he's saying. It also makes me realize that I haven't thought about my future or college much. I'm not sure what I want to do.

What do I want from life? It's the ultimate question, but who has the answer at sixteen? Certainly not me.

Do I even want to go to college? Do I want a career in boring business? Do I want a white picket fence and kids?

I need to start thinking about this, because what I do now will determine my future. One thing I know for sure —I want to be an artist. It might not bring in a lot of money, but I will be rich with the love of my passion.

When we pull up to our houses, I see Roman perched beside his motorcycle on the grass. It's black and chrome. He looks like a bad boy biker. I'd found it interesting he wears such heavy black boots, but now they make sense. I guess he rides to school each day.

"Thanks for the lift," I tell Jace as I jump out.

"No worries. If you need one tomorrow morning, I'll be here. Just text me."

I walk away from the car and toward my front door, the interactions I had with the guys today playing out in my head. It's all been so *normal.*

Maybe Asher is wrong? Maybe girls and guys can be friends without sex getting in the way.

But when I look back at Roman, who is following me...*fuck.* There's no way sex won't get in the way.

❮❮❮❯ ❮❯ ❮❮❯❯

"**D**o you think you'll go to college? Or want a future in football?" Dad asks Roman at the dinner table. Dad ordered Chinese, and it's been kinda funny watching him talk with Roman.

Roman barely said a word to me while we studied. At first, I thought he didn't understand the assignment, so he didn't have anything to say. But as I watched him write down his answers, I realized that wasn't the case. He's just quiet. Like when I first met him.

Well, he was quiet until Dad came home and asked him about a hundred questions. Roman hasn't missed a beat. It's jarring how he can be so closed off with me. Yet, in my dad's presence, he's open and even laughed. I'd had no idea he could do that still.

I've decided to make it my mission to hear that laugh again. Because it was deep and real.

"Okay, Dad, no more questions. We have lots of work to do. Football and everything else gets in the way, and we don't want to fail."

That had Dad pushing away from the table and clearing it. "No, you're right. Go study more. I'll clean up here."

I get up and Roman follows. Our books and my laptop are on the coffee table, but I know Dad likes to watch game tapes after dinner, so I gather up as much as I can. Roman follows my lead and grabs his stuff, and I lead him up to my room.

He hesitates at the door, which is funny. It's not like he's never been in here before. Far from it. He's had sleepovers in here with me more times than I can count.

Sometimes, he'd slept in the spare room Dad set up if

the boys ever wanted to sleep over and not be in the same room as me. That only happened a few times, and it was Hunter who slept in there the most. He said I snore loudly, but I think it's an excuse because he sometimes had nightmares and would wake me. He would thrash around and call out, and I would wake him and comfort him as best I could. He would cry himself to sleep, and the next day he would go home as soon as he got up. He was embarrassed by the nightmares, but he didn't have to be. I wanted to be there for him when he needed me.

Sitting down, I place my books on the floor, spreading them out around me. "Okay, we're gonna get as much of this done as possible."

I don't want to take up too much of his time outside of school. He has his job at the tattoo place downtown; I got that much out of him. Apart from that, he seems to not have much free time. So, we'll have one more study session next week, and that's all. I don't mind doing most the work, but he made it clear he doesn't want that. He wants to put in his share of the workload. I like that.

When Roman doesn't sit beside me, I look over and find him looking at one of my many sketch pads. Oh, fuck. I scramble up, my book and pen dropping to the floor as I reach over to grab it from him.

But he sees me coming and turns before I can reach the pad.

"You still draw?" he asks.

I try to reach around him without touching him, but he turns. I curse at how tall and wide he has gotten. I jump onto my bed and bounce slightly as I hold my hand out to him and cock my head. "Excuse me, you can't just come in here and look at my things."

He cocks his head and gives me a smirk. It's enough for me to drop my hand.

"Before you left, you drew me a daisy and gave it to me."

How could I forget? That was the day I rode my bike to his house and kissed him. I give him a small smile, hoping he isn't going to ask about the first kiss. No one has brought it again, and I hope to keep that buried. For at least fifty years.

"Yeah?" I reply hesitantly when he doesn't elaborate.

He grabs the back of his gray tee, and in one move, it's up and over his head and on my floor. *Fuck…Roman.*

Does he even know how hot that move is? I bite my lip as my eyes roll over his chest. He's covered in tattoos here too. These are a little different from his sleeve, and the one that catches my eye is the one over his heart.

"Holy shit, Roman." I move to the edge of the bed, wobbling a little on the mattress. Up here, I'm taller than him, and I like it. I have the urge to run my fingers through his long hair. I love the way it curls up at the ends. Maybe he will let me braid it before the game on Friday?

"Jeanie," I whisper. It's his Mom's name. Under my daisy. It looks exactly like the daisy that I drew for him. Unlike the rest of his ink, there's no color. It's just a penciled drawing of a daisy bending over slightly. One that a twelve-year-old girl drew for her best friend, because she knew she wouldn't be picking daisies with him anymore.

"Wow, Roman." I'm choked up. He tattooed my drawing onto his body.

I study his whole chest while he stands there, looking at anything other than me. There are marks, scars, and old, yellowing bruises mixed in with purple ones on his ribs.

There are round scars that are puckered and old, but they're there. The tattoos can't hide everything.

My throat thickens with sadness. I know where he got the round scars. I'd seen one on him before I left, and he told me not to worry about it.

I should have called him every day. I should have told my dad to save him, take him in. I feel a tear slip down my cheek, but I don't wipe it away. I should have done so much to protect him, and I couldn't. Now, he's a broken man at the age of sixteen, and I blame myself. He wouldn't have turned out like this if I'd been there for him. I know it.

My fingers reach out to touch the most visible scar beside the daisy, and he takes a step back. I bring my hand back to my chest just as fast.

"Sorry," I whisper.

He turns and puts his shirt on. On his back, the scars are even worse, and I look away, blinking back the tears. I don't want him to see pity on my face. I know he's too proud for that. He can't think living with his dad is safe? He needs somewhere safe to go.

"Do you want to stay here tonight?" I find myself asking before I've even spoken with my dad. But I know if I tell my dad what I saw, he'll make Roman move in here in a heartbeat.

Roman turns around and shakes his head, grabbing his books off the floor as I stand there, not knowing what to do or say. Fuck. I shouldn't have tried to touch him.

"No, I need to get going."

"Work?" I question, thinking it's the answer he'll feel most comfortable with.

In reality, we both know he's running away because he let down a wall with me tonight, and I overstepped by trying to push him on the touching thing. I keep forgetting he's not the same boy I left. No hugs or smiles. It breaks my heart.

Roman just grunts and leaves the room, closing the door behind him.

I slump down on my bed and pull my knees to my chest and sob.

Oh, Roman. What has happened to you, my sweet hugger?

TWENTY-SEVEN
MILA

"Tonight's the big game. How do you think you'll do?" I ask Jace as he taps away to the beat of the old rock song he's been listening to each morning. He seems nervous.

"We are gonna win, there isn't a doubt."

He looks over at me with that grin he wears. Each time I see it, it brings my mind back to that moment in his room, and heat flares all over my body. Fuck, I can't keep thinking about that. It's not gonna happen again. We're friends now. That's what I asked for. Nothing is gonna happen again.

His abs tensing as ropes of his cum hit them…oh, god, I have a problem. Or I'm really needing to rub one out, because *fuck*, I have sex on the brain.

Friends with benefits?

Oh, god, why does that even pop into my head? I can't do that. Hell, with how much the three of *them* fought over the first kiss thing, I'm pretty sure having sex with one would blow up way worse than that.

Grady has artfully avoided me since that kiss in his car

on Monday. I confronted him about it yesterday. He said he isn't avoiding me, but we need to keep the kiss to ourselves. No telling anyone, he wants to be the one to tell him. If it comes up. That sounds fair enough to me. Jace has been amazing this week, and I don't want anything to rock the boat. I have my best friend back.

Grady has been busy getting extra workouts in and studying heaps with Makai. He's tutoring Grady in some of his classes. I'm failing Algebra already, and I'm tempted to ask if Makai will help me too.

The halls are alive with red as we enter the school. Girls run to Jace and giggle; cheerleaders are kinda annoying. But I press past them and ignore Jace calling out for me to wait up. He needs to address his fan club. I'm sure he'll want to party with one of them later now that he's single.

Britney hasn't been taking their breakup well. Yesterday, she threw a tampon at me. It wasn't used, so that was a good start. I shoved her slightly, and she fell over a trash can. It fell on her, and some of the garbage tipped out onto her. She screamed at the sight of a banana peel touching her leg.

I'm waiting for her to come at me harder now. I think the days of the PG version mean girl of Britney are over. So, I came prepared with extra clothes in my bag. I've been trying to think of what she might do next. I'm thinking a drink or something spilled on me. Or she takes my clothes while I'm in the shower after PE.

Either way, I'm prepared. But I'm not prepared for anything else, so I hope she doesn't get too creative.

"Hey, Mila."

I turn to see Hunter jogging toward me. A few girls call out his name as he passes them. He slings his arm around my shoulder and leads me to my locker. I can't stop myself from breathing him in. He smells so good. Much better than his gym bag.

"So, you gonna cheer me on tonight? I'll be looking for you up in the stands...wearing red."

I hit his side playfully, and he fakes a painful groan.

Shaking my head, I laugh. "I'll be cheering on the whole team. Not just you, Hunter."

I get to my locker, and he leans against the one beside it as I open mine, pulling books out of my bag and placing them on the shelf.

"Hey, Hunter," a girl practically purrs from behind me.

I know that voice—it's Summer Waters.

"Yeah?" He sounds bored when he answers. His eyes are still on me, and my lip twitches.

"You going to the party after the game? It's at Zack's."

Hunter grunts. "I know where it is, Summer. He's my teammate, and it's a football party. Are you going to be there?"

I spin to see her batting her lashes at him with a flirty smile. I roll my eyes. Come on, really? I find myself clenching my teeth. Who does she think she is?

But, deep down, a flare of jealously sparks. Even though he doesn't seem interested, she doesn't stop. I don't want him with her. She isn't good enough for him. No one is.

"Yeah, I'll be waiting for you." She reaches out to touch him, and he pulls away before she can make contact. She makes a sad sound, and I snort. Her eyes bore into me, and I try to cover my smile by looking away.

But Hunter catches my eye and grins. "You're gonna be waiting a long time, because if you're there, I'm not going." I close my locker, and he swings his arm around me again. "I'm gonna be wherever Mila is."

The look Summer gives me is a warning of what's to come later. *Thanks for painting an extra target on my back, Hunter.* But I can handle her. Hell, she's Britney's best friend, and so far, their attempts to hurt or humiliate me have been so sad that I don't think they understand how that looks on them.

He looks down at me with that stupid, sexy smile of his, showing off his perfect teeth. Summer stomps her foot and storms off.

"So, where are you gonna be tonight, Mila?" he asks.

I duck from under his arm and pull away. I turn, walking backward, watching his brow rise at the move.

"Home alone."

He cocks his head.

"Not alone?" I ask.

He chuckles. "I will see you there."

◆◆◆

At lunch, I meet Roman outside where he's been every day this week. Jace and Hunter sit with the other footballer players. They don't ask me to sit with them or come out to sit with us. It's like they know Roman needs his space, and he needs it with me. Like this is our private time, and I love it.

"Hey, what ya doing?" I ask as I pull up my ass beside his. I keep a small space between us, as I know he doesn't like me touching him. And I don't want to accidently touch him if I'm too close.

"Thinking," he replies, looking up at the blue sky, squinting at the sunlight.

His hair drapes over his eyes and face as he turns to look at me. I smile, and the corner of his lip lifts. He pushes his hair back, and it falls down again.

I laugh. "Can I braid your hair?" I ask.

I've wanted to do it all week. He has an undercut that's super short, but he keeps it long on top. I want to give him Viking braids. I think that would look hot on him. Plus, he has the cheekbones and jawline to pull that off. He has some blond stubble on his jaw today, like he didn't shave this morning. I really want to run my finger along his skin and feel the short bristles, but I don't.

"No," he says in a monotone voice, but he doesn't take his eyes from me.

"Please? It will help you play tonight if your hair isn't in your face."

"I tie it up for the game."

I let out a huff and take a bite of my sandwich. I don't speak, just sit here quietly while he eats beside me. I can feel him looking at me, but I don't acknowledge it. I pretend to ignore him and take a sip of Coke.

"How does this braid work?" he asks, and I try hide my smile, but I can't. I've found that when he says no, I just need to wait. He'll change his mind.

"Well, I brought hair ties, so I can do three, and they'll look really cool." He appears skeptical, and I chuckle. "I promise they'll make you look cool."

He mutters under his breath, "I'm already cool."

And I burst out laughing.

I love moments like this with Roman. I like that he's letting me in a little. That he trusts me enough to talk to me. We're still far from what we used to be, but slow steps are better than none. What's that saying? Slow and steady wins the race. I'm going with that plan of attack with Roman.

"So, I can give you braids?"

He grunts and nods.

I'd been hoping he would say yes. I have a comb, spray bottle with water, hairspray, and hair ties in a bag sitting beside me. When I start to pull the items out, I hear him chuckle just a little to himself. Like he knew I was gonna get my way no matter what. The sound of his chuckle makes me feel like I'm floating on cloud nine.

I stand up behind him, and he stiffens. "I'm only gonna touch your hair," I whisper, and I see the tension leave his shoulders. I start running the comb through his tangles and I snicker. "How often do you brush your hair?"

He shrugs.

It's not too bad, but there are enough knots in there to make me think he only brushes it once a month. He grunts as I comb out all the tangles and knots.

I separate it into three parts, and I hum to myself. "Can you hold this?" When I place the comb in front of his face, he reaches up and takes it.

"Thanks." I grab my spray bottle and wet his hair, making it damp and easy to braid. When I do mine, this is the easiest way.

I start with the first section in the middle, and it comes out perfect. "Yes, looking awesome," I say more to myself then to Roman as I dance a little on the spot.

"How often do you braid people's hair?" he asks as I gesture for the comb.

He hands it up to me, and I start on one of the side braids. "Never. But I promise I'm an expert."

And that gets a deep chuckle out of him. A warm

feeling bursts through me. I'm making him laugh, and I don't have to do much for it.

It doesn't take long before it's all done, and I'm kind of sad. I love touching his hair, and the fact that he let me touch it makes my heart soar. I come around to his front and study my work.

Roman looks up at me, and I can't wipe the smile from my face.

"Looks good?" he asks.

I clap my hands and nod. Pulling my phone out of my pocket, I bring it up to take a photo. He doesn't move or smile, but he doesn't tell me I can't take one. I snap a quick photo then show it to him.

He runs his hand over the braids as he peers at the photo. "They look fantastic, Mila."

I giggle. "I told you I was an expert."

He stands up and hands me my phone back. The bell rings as I look down at the photo. God, I wish he could see how handsome he is.

A large, warm body surrounds me, and I freeze. I turn my face and it snuggles...into Roman's chest. My heart starts to race. He's hugging me. I don't know what to do. I want to hug him back, but I'm scared he'll pull away if I touch him.

I slowly raise one of my hands and place it gently on his side. He lets out a deep breath. "Thank you," he whispers low, and I smile into his chest.

"Thank you for being my guinea pig, Roman."

He chuckles again as he pulls away. God, will I ever want to stop listening to his laugh? Unlikely. It's so Roman.

"Anytime, Mila." He smiles and walks off, leaving me to gather my thoughts and supplies.

◄▓► ◄▓► ◄▓►

'm on a high when I meet Ella and Daniel outside their house. They're taking me to the game tonight. I'm wearing the jersey Hunter gave me...after I washed it, of course. It isn't like the one Jace had changed me into last Saturday; that one smelled like his cologne and him. Hunter's smelled like feet.

Jace and Grady's parents are the best. They greet me with huge hugs, and Ella kisses my head and calls me her long-lost daughter.

"We need to have you over for dinner next week, Mila. We've missed you so much," Ella says from the front seat of the car.

Getting a lift with the Monteros is so much better than being stuck on a bus with a bunch of other students.

"Sounds great to me. Just tell me what day suits you both."

"How does Monday sound to you? The boys finish at six, but I'll be home just before to start dinner. You can come over, and we can talk about girl stuff, like makeup, clothes, and *boys*."

I laugh at the way she says *boys*.

"Sounds perfect. I'll come over early to help you."

We sit together at the game. Since Sadie and Cadence still aren't into football, just the players, I don't have anyone else to sit with. But I'm grateful to have Ella and Daniel with me. They always treated me like I was their daughter, and they still do. Daniel makes sure we get to our seats before he takes off to buy us hot dogs and soda.

"The boys look great this year," I hear someone tell Daniel as he takes a seat next to Ella. Another says the same thing, and I love the way he beams at the praise for his boys.

It's true. They do look good. *At football*...football is what I meant. Yep, good at football.

I find the three of them on the field. I'd put my hair in pigtails, and I twirl the strands of one side through my fingers. I'd be lying if I said I'm not nervous. I want the boys to win so badly. I really believe I'm part of the reason they lost last week, and I don't want to do that to them ever again. Especially now that we're all friends again.

Plus, I know how much Jace needs a football scholarship. I assume Hunter won't? His dad will probably send him somewhere big and pompous. Roman, I haven't spoken to about it. But with how well he plays, he could get a scholarship. If he wants to go to college, that is.

Hunter looks up at me, and I smile. He found me in the sea of red. I wave down at him. He smirks, taps his chest, and kisses his fingers and points to me. I laugh and shake my head at him, my cheeks flushing.

"OMG, dork," I mutter to myself. But the butterflies in my stomach tell me I liked that a little too much.

"Are you and Hunter a thing?" Ella asks from beside me.

Oh, God. She saw that?

I turn to her, my cheeks still warm. Shit, I'm blushing; that's going to be hard to explain. I put a hand on my cheek and shake my head no, but I can't wipe the smile off my face at what he just did. She raises her brows and gives me a knowing smile.

"No, no. Not a thing. Nope...not at all. I'm not seeing anyone." I think I said *no* a little too many times in that sentence.

Not knowing what else to say, I turn back and look

down at the guys again. It doesn't help because, when I see the three of them standing together now, talking and laughing, my heart does a summersault.

I want them all. I want to kiss them, hug them, and have them ask how my day was. I want them to look at me like I'm the first and last person they think about every day.

Roman catches my eye, and the grin he gives me almost sets me on fire. I put my hand to my chest to stop my heart from leaping out and running down there to claim him as mine in front of everyone. Jace is slower to turn, and he winks over at me with a slow, sexy smirk that hits me low, deep in my belly. I'm wet, and my nipples are hard and achy.

Fuck.

Girls can't be friends with guys. That's al there is to it.

Sex is definitely getting in the way now. I have no idea how I'm going to handle this. I've resisted the flirty banter with Hunter all week. It's been fun, and I might have gotten a little swept up in it because I wanted it. I don't want him to stop and try it on someone else. I want all this attention; I want all of Jace's and Roman's too. I'm greedy, I know.

I'm excited that Hunter's coming over to my place after the game. But I'd ended up inviting Roman and Jace too. Having them there would stop me from doing something I shouldn't with Hunter.

But that's a lie.

I want to do things—bad things—with all of them.

TWENTY-EIGHT
HUNTER

We won.

I knew we would, but this has been an incredible night for the Rebels. Something happened to Roman; he's a different person tonight. Might have been the smile he was wearing when the guys all commented on his hair and how wicked it looked. Or the person who did it for him made him smile that way.

I'd watched her earlier from where I sat inside at lunch. I don't know if Mila realizes, but she bites her lower lip when she concentrates, and, hell, that destroys my concentration. I've seen her doing that a lot in art, and I have to readjust my cock each time. Hell, even now I'm getting hard just thinking about it. The teacher has commented that I'm behind in my work, but that's because I'm too busy staring at a work of art.

Mila Hart.

Tonight, seeing her up there, cheering and screaming out to us, made me want to show off. She called my name. and I heard her over the rest of the crowd. I'd never run so fast in my life. I was worried I would miss the catch, but I caught it, digging my heels in and running for her. Getting the touchdown for her. I played better than ever, and it's because she was there.

I know Roman played for her too. He might say he doesn't want her, but I know he does. He wants her approval. He wants her to see him how she used to. Nothing's changed for her either. She still watches him like she always did. Reading his face and body language and knowing what to say at the right time.

Jace, on the other hand, cocky bastard.

He changed when we got to high school. Freshman year, he shot up out of nowhere and decided to be the leader of our trio. I never fought for it. Mila had always been our leader. Wherever she went, we followed. No one ever called her that, but she was always the one who spoke up for us first. She was the first to get into fights to protect us.

So, when Jace claimed her spot, I didn't give a shit. I was happy to go along with whatever he wanted, as long as I was having fun and getting pussy. I'd followed Jace and let him lead.

But, tonight, his passes were on point. His calls, everything. He didn't miss a beat. If there were any scouts out there, I can bet they all wrote his name down. Roman too, even though he's made it clear that college isn't gonna happen. He plans to work at the tattoo shop with Ronnie after high school.

At least he can make that choice for himself. My dad's still breathing down my neck about wanting me to go to Lakeview Prep. But as long as I keep my grade up, he can't force me to move. We signed a contract.

Grady had an off night for the first time ever; he hasn't been the same since we had our fight on Monday. I'm not sure if it's Jace or all three of us he has a problem with, but he's hardly spoken to us.

We're almost back at school, and my heart is racing. I can't wait to see Mila.

When she said she was going to be home alone, then not alone, I'd hoped she was trying to tell me something. Hell, she was flirting with me, but she had been all week. So, when I said I would meet her there, and she didn't question it, I thought for sure she wants to be alone with me. Tonight is the night I'll tell her I want to be more than friends.

God, I've never just wanted to be her friend. I have always wanted more. But now that the carrot has been dangled, I want to take a bite. Jace agreed on Monday that the pact is null and void. We just had to promise not to fight with each other when she picks one of us.

If she doesn't pick me, I'll be devastated. But I'll try and be happy for whoever she does pick. Try...not to smash them in the face with my fist every day.

I made the rule that there's no talking about it. If Jace gets her, I don't want to hear how amazing her kisses are or how good she makes him feel. We all agreed on that. That's how I know Roman isn't over her; he wants to kiss her again.

He's just scared. The fighting down at The Shed would have to stop if he did have her. The people down there are scary motherfuckers, and that's no place for Mila. Hell, that's no place for my friend, but I can't stop him.

I saw her blush tonight when I blew her a kiss from the field. And every time I turned to look at her, she was beaming. It felt good to have her looking at me like that. Hell, I have wanted her since I was a kid. Now, tonight.

It's finally my chance. My chance to have her alone and tell her how I have fallen in love with her, again.

Not that I ever fell out of love with her. She might have broken my heart when she left, but that's history now. I don't want to waste time being upset over that. Hell, I don't even care if I was the last one she kissed before she left. I want to move forward with Mila, and I hope this means she does too.

I haven't said shit to the guys about where I'm going after the game. I'm hoping Jace is going to Zack's party so he won't see my car out in front of Mila's. But I look down at the group message on my phone and realize Jace has started a new chat...with the four of us, called "blood friends."

I run my thumb over my scar; there will only ever be four of us who understand what that means. It would be creepy for someone who didn't know what that meant to see it.

Mila: Can you come over at 11:30? Dad's coming home to get some stuff before going to Kate's, and I don't want to explain to him about the three of you staying over at my house.

The fuck?

Jace turns where he is seated next to me on the bus. "My parents will be in bed, but you can come hang in my room until then."

I'm just...I don't know what to think. He ignores my silence and glances past me across the aisle. "You too, Roman."

This isn't how I expected my night to go at all. All my plans have gone out the window. We've been in Jace's room for about twenty minutes already, and I haven't sat down. I'm trying to figure out how this is gonna work. How to play this out now that they're both gonna be there.

Roman's lying on Jace's bed with his eyes closed and his hands behind his head. He still has the braids Mila gave him. I don't think he will take them out until he has to wash his hair. He has a peaceful look on his face, and I can't begrudge the guy for wanting to go over to Mila's. Not when he has been more himself this past week than he has in four years.

Jace looks out the window again to see if James has left. He's looked almost every minute. I can tell he's eager to get over there, and it frustrates me. I can't sit here and watch this. I pace beside the bedroom door.

"Seriously, Hunter, what's up?" Jace asks as he closes the blinds again, turning to me.

I shrug. I can't tell them I'm upset they're coming, that she invited me first. But did I just go and invite myself read the signal wrong? It's not fair to take it out on Jace and Roman. It's my fault.

"No, tell me what's up with you. You've been pacing since we got in my room. James is still there. We have to wait like she asked. What more can I do other than go over and demand he leave his own house so three guys can have a sleepover with his daughter?"

He thinks that's why I'm pacing. At least he hasn't clued into the real reason. I've been trying to figure out how to get her alone once we get into her house. I want to talk to her in private and tell her how I feel. Fuck, putting my heart on the line like that makes my stomach turn. Normally, I don't care if I'm rejected by a girl. It doesn't happen often, and there is always another one there, waiting for me.

But I don't think I can handle being rejected by Mila. I don't want another girl.

I want her.

The sound of a car door has Jace looking out the window again. like a creepy fucker.

"Shit, man, at least wait until he's gone before spying on him. He might see you and change his mind about leaving," I grumble at Jace.

He doesn't respond.

Roman rolls off the bed, and we both go to the window to see for ourselves that James is leaving. We see the headlights of her dad's truck as it pulls out of the driveway.

"Oh, shit," Jace utters under his breath, and my eyes are drawn to Mila's room. Fucker gets to stare into her room any time he wants, and tonight, I mutter the exact same words.

"Oh, shit. Does she realize we can see her?" I ask, but it's more to myself than them. I hear something clatter on the windowsill as Jace grabs a walkie-talkie. Oh, wow, that's the one they used as kids. He switches it on, and we're greeted by white noise and a beep.

Mila pauses and looks around her room. My brows rise as she goes to her windowsill and picks up her walkie-talkie before looking over to us. Her eyes widen slightly, then she smiles and winks at us. God, I can feel that smile and wink down into my cock. But it's not just that; it's everything.

"Someone putting on a show for us?" Jace says down the line to her.

She grins on the other end and takes a step back. She's wearing a black lace bra and a thong again. When she spins, I can see her perky, smooth ass, and I do everything in my power to hold back my raging hard-on. But it's impossible when she looks so fine, and I just know she's everything I ever wanted. Like every Christmas gift all wrapped into one sexy, smart, and sassy girl next door.

"Don't take too long jerking each other off. I have popcorn and beer."

God, she's playing us. She did that on purpose. Knew we would be looking.

Well, I want to be the first to tell her how much I liked her show, and I want to see it up close and personal. I move away from the window, rearrange my junk, and grab my bag. I run out of Jace's house like it's on fire. I want to be the first one to see her and maybe catch her still wearing only that black lace.

I'm coming, Mila Hart...just hopefully not in my shorts.

TWENTY-NINE
MILA

knew they were waiting at Jace's. I'm not stupid; it's why I turned the light on when I came into the room after my shower. I quickly slipped my underwear on and put on a little show. I wanted to see what would happen, and their responses didn't disappoint.

Thank you, Victoria's Secret.

I'm surprised that my walkie-talkie works after all these years. I'd turned it on in hopes that Jace might wanna talk to me during the week, but he never did. I'd forgotten about it and left it on the windowsill. I had my phone with me, thinking they might text. Turns out, all I needed to do for him to pick it up was show a little bit of black lace.

I hear footsteps barreling through the house and look up just in time to see Hunter burst into my room as I'm doing up the last button on my silk pajamas. He stumbles forward, and I laugh. As he rights himself, breathing hard, and takes me all in, his face falls a little at my now dressed body. It seems he really wanted to catch me here in my underwear, and that sends little bolts of pleasure to my core. I'm glad he is just as worked up as I get with him.

"How the hell did you get—"

He holds up the spare key. I reach out, snatching it from him, and he laughs.

"You were quick...I hope you're not always that quick." I wink before turning around and bending over to grab my oversize wool cardigan from my bed.

It's becoming cooler at night, but I wanted to wear this outfit to bed, in front of them all. Because I know it's sexy. And well...I'm having thoughts of the wicked variety. I want one of them to make the first move. I feel like it's the best way if I'm not the one choosing. Because I can't. They can all chose me.

Hunter's fingers grip my hips and curl around them. I brace my hands on the bed to steady myself, because if I turn around, I will kiss him right now, and I can't. I can't make the first move. His body moves in, and he grounds his erection into my ass. I press back a little, and he moans.

He breathes out my name in a caress, and my nipples tighten as I slowly arch back to standing. His body is warm and large against my back. His hand comes around to my tummy, pulling me close to him. My breathing grows rapid, anticipation of what he's going to do next making me tremble with need.

"God, Mila. You're killing me. Every day, I dream of touching you like this. Feeling you like this. And now..." he whispers into my throat as I feel his tongue trace a line up the side of my throat to the shell of my ear. "Now you can feel what you do to me." His hips buck into me harder, and I can feel how hard he is for me.

My ass presses back into his erection, and a need for him to claim me pulsates between my legs. I clamp them together, wanting and needing to be touched there. His hand on my belly starts to lower, and I can feel how wet I am. I want him to feel that too.

I hear the other two making their way up the stairs and calling out Hunter's name. They aren't happy that he's still faster than them.

We separate like we've just been caught with our hands in the cookie jar. Hell, Hunter almost had his hand in my cookie jar.

"I wasn't going to do that," he murmurs.

I cock my head, and he chuckles, running his hand over the back of his neck.

"Okay that's a lie, but I wasn't going to do it so quickly is what I meant. I was going to talk to you first, but you got me all worked up."

I laugh and shake my head, making my way past Hunter. I pause, looking up at him under my lashes. He looks down and licks his lips. I run my fingers down his chest, stopping right as they reach the waist band of his basketball shorts.

"Let's watch movies." I wink up at him, and he lets out a deep groan.

I move my fingers slowly lower to see what other reactions I can get out of him before the other two show up. He grabs my wrist before I can touch his hard cock that's tenting in his shorts. He lets out a chuckle, shaking his head with a grin.

"Wicked girl. I can't sit and watch movies with cum in my shorts."

I laugh as he lets go of my wrist, and I take the few steps to my doorway to see Jace rounding the stairs. He hasn't seen what happened, but I bet he can see the flush on my cheeks.

I grin at him. "Let's watch movies. I picked a few good ones."

Just before I head down the stairs, I turn back to Hunter. The heel of his hand is pressing down on his erection. He catches me looking, and I wink.

He throws his head back and lets out a pained groan.

'm not watching that." Jace points to the screen where I have *The Notebook* lined up on Netflix.

I pout, and he shakes his head, but he has a hint of a smile he tries to hide by taking a swig from the bottle of beer I got for us. Yeah…I got beer for tonight. Not a lot, just twelve.

I said I wouldn't drink being back here, but this is different. I feel safe with the three of them. I don't have to worry about them taking advantage of me. Hell, I want them all to touch me, and I need a cold shower after what happened with Hunter in my room. I'm still all worked up over the way he touched me.

Asher has been apologizing to me all week over the whole hand on his junk thing. I told him to get me beer and all will be forgiven. Not that it hasn't already been. He made a good point with his erection.

I don't just want to be friends with my guys. I want tonight to be fun and sexy. I want us to be like old times… but with beer and a romantic movie and my little silk shorts.

I need to cool myself down. I feel hot and needy, and we haven't even started the movie. I shuck the cardigan I put on while walking down the stairs. I was warm before putting it on, but I'd been trying to hide my reaction to Hunter from Jace.

"Okay, we can watch it," Jace says quickly, looking at my chest.

I glance down and find my nipples hard still. I look over to Hunter and he tips his bottle of beer toward me and winks.

Jace chuckles. "You don't play fair, Hart."

"When did I ever play fair?" I tease back as I place a bowl of popcorn on the coffee table.

"When we were all your first kiss."

It's like a bucket of cold water washes over me. I stumble over the rug and peer at Jace. Is he bringing that up again to hurt me? Is he going to press me again about who was first?

"Really? Jace, you had to go there?" Hunter says as he comes over and glares at his friend, standing beside me in a protective stance.

Roman even comes to stand beside me, and we all look down to where Jace is perched on edge of the sofa's arm.

Jace puts his hands up. "No, fuck. I'm just saying… ugh. I finally get it, okay? No matter the order, we all wanted to be her first kiss, and we were. She made it fair in the only way she could."

"Okay," I say after having a moment to process it. I'm not sure if I believe he's truly okay with not knowing the order. But when he gives me those big, brown, pleading eyes, I smile and reach out to him.

He takes my hand. "Sorry, I didn't mean to upset you."

I nod and hug him. He's easier to hug from where he's sitting, and he wraps his arms around me. He smells good, and it's easy to forgive him.

I break away from the hug as Hunter grabs the remote

and lays down on the sofa bed I pulled out earlier. I told Dad I was gonna watch movies and sleep down here. He didn't question it. The problem is, it's only big enough for two, and with three big football players and me, there isn't enough room for us all.

"You sure you don't want to watch that shades of grey movie, Mila? I heard it's romantic too." Hunter winks over at me, and I laugh.

"You want to watch *Fifty Shades of Grey* with your best friends? Are you sure?"

Roman snorts and coughs from where he sits in the armchair. The no touching rule is still in place. He didn't hug me when he saw me before, and I wished he would. But I respect his boundaries. I will wait for him to come to me. I know he will. I just have to wait.

Jace drops on the sofa bed, and the springs make a horrible protest at his weigh.

Hunter snickers. "Fat ass, you're too heavy. Go sit in that chair. Mila can lay here, beside me." Hunter pats the spot between them.

Well, the lack of a spot is more like it. There's maybe two inches of space between them, if that. I will be touching them, all night.

Not gonna say no to that. Only a crazy person wouldn't want to be pressed between two hot guys. But I will have to keep my hands to myself.

"Okay, let me grab more popcorn and turn the light out."

I run to the kitchen and grab another bowl of popcorn and four more beers. Then, I make my way back, clicking the light switch with my elbow on the way past it.

"Shit, Mila." Jace moves over to help me put the beers down on the coffee table. They're cold, and the condensation leaves my white silk wet, where I'd hugged them to my chest as I carried them. You can see my black lace through it.

Jace sees it too, and his eyes linger for an extra beat. He licks his lips, and my skin prickles at his attention. He makes a small groaning sound as he grabs my waist and hauls me over between Hunter and himself. I reach out to get the popcorn, but he presses my shoulder back.

"Stay," he mumbles.

Halfway through the movie, I look over at Roman. He's fast asleep. Hunter draws circles with his thumb on my bare thigh, and the touch makes my center throb. Jace has been holding my hand for the past twenty minutes, his thumb running along the pulse point in my wrist.

This isn't how I planned tonight to go. Hell, I never really had a plan. All I know is, I want more than friendships with these guys, and I have no idea how to even broach the topic with them. Yep, I can be strong and sassy like Ella says, but telling the guys I want them all and won't share them with other girls...yeah, I don't have the guts to do that.

Each one means something different to me; they each fill a place in my heart. Without one or two of them, my heart won't ever be complete. I've never considered dating more than one person. I always saw that as cheating. But if they all know, it would be okay, right? If they all agree.

I have no idea how to make that happen. They would have to share me, my time, my heart with two others. I roll my head toward Jace and close my eyes, taking a deep breath as I settle deeper. I'm so sleepy, I can't fight it.

Hunter and Jace speak in whispered voices. Their deep rumbles sooth me, and I curl up tighter to Jace. My ass is up against Hunter's hip, and I feel him run his hand over my silk shorts.

"All's fair in love and war," Jace says.

"There is no war, we agreed. We also have to accept that she might pick someone outside the three of us. Like Emerson," Hunter replies.

Emerson? No, he doesn't give me butterflies like they do.

There's a moment of silence before Hunter speaks again.

"Who gives you butterflies, Mila?"

I tense at his words. "Did I say that out loud?"

"Yes," they both reply, a low chuckle coming from Hunter.

"Tell us," Jace adds.

I smile sleepily. "You."

"Who?" they both ask, and I feel the bed jostle as they move, my warm bubble growing colder.

"Which one, Mila?" Hunter probes.

I roll onto my back and yawn and stretch. I don't mean to. I just need to. They both groan at the movement. I can feel my pajama top ride up, exposing my bare stomach. I smile sleepily.

"You're killing us here, babe. Which one?" Jace asks.

One of them runs their fingers over my belly, and I feel it everywhere.

I open my eyes to see them both looking down at me. Hunter's hand is hovering over my belly. I look over to Roman. He's not sleeping anymore—his eyes are on me.

"All of you."

THIRTY
JACE

"Die, fuckers." Mila jumps on the edge of my bed, a controller in one hand and a fist in the air. God, she's sexy, even when she's a gloating winner.

"Oh my god, Mila. You're blood thirsty," Grady teases from beside her. His character dies dramatically on the screen. I'd invited her over to play on the Xbox with me after Coach let us go for the day. It had been nice to watch game tapes of myself when I'd played the best fucking game of my life.

Only, Grady took it upon himself to join us, like a third wheel. What's more annoying is that Mila thought it was a great idea.

It's "how we used to be," she'd said. Which isn't true. Grady used to avoid Mila, like he had been for the past week. Now, all of a sudden, he's in her face again and pissing me off. When she bumps his shoulder, he looks at her like she's the best thing ever, and I crack my knuckles. His eyes are drawn to me now, and I glare at him.

"Don't you have something better to do? Like see

Makai and study or some shit?" Anything but be here, in my room.

Grady just laughs. "I don't study all the time, Jace. It's good to have some fun." He bumps Mila's shoulder back, and she giggles.

I grit my teeth and clench my fist, trying to hold in everything I want to say to him, so I don't look like a totally prick in front of Mila. But when Mila leaves, I'm going to break his nose.

She is leaving in ten minutes, so Grady better be ready to run. Her dad's taking her out to dinner with Asher and his mom and sister. I was thinking of going to a party and waiting for her to get home. But she's not sure if she's staying over at Asher's. And even though they say they're only friends, I don't like it. I don't trust him not to make a move on my girl.

Yeah, my girl.

I give her butterflies. She said that last night. Yeah, we all do, but I know I have to be the one to give her the most butterflies and orgasms. Hell, maybe if Grady wasn't here right now, I would be able to convince Mila to go for another round of playtime like last Saturday. But this time, I'd get to taste her.

Fuck, even the thought of her licking my cum off her finger gets me hard. Everything about this girl does. I might have been angry at her when she first came back. Hell, finding out my first kiss isn't what I'd thought had upset me more than anything.

But I've settled on the fact that the way she gave us each her first kiss is fair. It's not important who was really first. Still, a little bit of me wants to know. Maybe, one day, she will tell us. Right now, that's not important. What's important is Grady getting a clue and fucking off.

"I actually better go. I need to grab some things from my room before I leave." She squeezes my knee as she stands up. But she does the same to Grady, and my pulse speeds up. My fist, his nose, as soon as she walks out that door.

"Thanks for a good afternoon, boys. I wanna play that again. I like kicking your butts." She smiles and wraps her arms around me.

What she doesn't know is I've been playing badly so she would win. Nothing makes me happier than watching her win. She is a boastful winner and loves to rub it in the loser's face.

Maybe next time, I will bet her a piece of clothing every time I win...I like where that thought came from.

I hug her back and she turns. Grady is standing now, and she hesitates for a moment before hugging him. I don't like the smile on his face or the fact that she's touching him.

I shove his shoulder, wanting him to let go of her. "She needs to go now, or she will be late," I explain when Mila's eyes turn on me, questioning.

"That was a little pushy, Jace."

"I didn't want you to be late." I give her my all-American boy-next-door smile. She doesn't fall for it.

She just shakes her head. "Talk to you both later."

I punch Grady in the shoulder the moment she leaves the house. He steps back, holding his shoulder and looking at me like he can't believe I just did that.

"What the fuck is your problem, Jace?"

"You know what the fuck my problem is. You could have left us alone. I wasn't gonna spend the whole afternoon gaming. I had other plans, and they didn't involve you."

His mouth opens then closes. He runs his hand through his hair and shakes his head. "She picked you?" His voice is deeper than usual, like he can't believe she would pick me.

"No, not yet. I was going to help her with her choosing process, but you cock-blocked me all afternoon."

"What the hell happened to 'the pact stands'? You don't care that making a move on Mila is going to destroy your two best friends? Do you really want that? For you or for her?"

I shake my head. "No, that won't happen. We agreed, each man for himself and to be happy with the one she picks. It's not going to destroy anything."

"Would you really be happy if she came to you right now, holding Hunter's hand, and told you that she wants to just be friends? That she picks Hunter?"

I growl lowly at that; that's not going to happen.

"Yeah, exactly my point. Have you guys thought about it, really?"

"We all discussed it after the fight. Makes sense. She's a big girl, and she can chose for herself. Roman's out. He made that clear. It's just me against Hunter."

"And you know how that sounds right now? You against Hunter. That's not how friends should be. Against each other is what enemies are made of. God, Jace. You can be thick at times, but you need to stop and think. This is the end of you all if you do this. The pact is the only thing that kept you together all those years."

I don't answer him. I know what he's saying. I get it. Fuck, I hate that he's right, but I just can't step back and watch the girl of my dreams with someone else. Does he even understand how hard that is? If he loved someone as much as I do Mila, he would get it.

Grady paces a by the door. Mom and Dad are home today. They can probably hear our fight but are ignoring it. Mom always says it's best to work it out ourselves but to come to them before fists are involved.

"Have you ever thought about others? Like, not Hunter and you. There are plenty of guys who would love to go out with Mila. Guys who have been crushing on her for years. What about them?"

"She said Emerson doesn't give her butterflies."

I'd always known it would just come down to the three of us; that's why the pact existed in the first place. Roman's out, Hunter's gone all in with the flirty shit, and the one who's gonna be standing at the end is me.

Mila is end game. She's the girl I'm going to marry. After college and everything, I will marry her and put babies in her belly and show everyone that she's mine. We will be together forever. I smile at the image in my head of her with her long blonde hair, a cute little kid with my hair and eyes on her hip, kissing me as I walk in the front door of our house.

"I kissed her."

I snap out of my daydream and look over at him, surprised by the expression of guilt on his face. Huh? What did he just say...?

"Jace, did you hear me? I said I kissed her. And she kissed me back." His hand rubs the back of his neck, and I can see it written all over his face. He didn't, she didn't, *no*.

"No, you're fucking with me." No way, I can't believe she kissed Grady...there's no way. And he wouldn't do that to me; he wouldn't kiss the girl I've been in love with since I could walk.

"I'm not fucking with you. Shit, I had a crush on her for years, okay? Just like all three of you did. I wasn't part of your pact, but I respected the rules and never made a move on her. Until last week."

I don't even blink. I just charge at my larger, older, line-backer brother and smash into him. He's prepared for it and doesn't fall over like I wanted. Motherfucker is strong. I should've known that, though. He's tackled me enough over the years.

"You're a fucking asshole. You knew I've loved her all these years, and you went and did that. You dirty bastard." I punch at his chest, his kidneys, and he blocks them all.

"I'm sorry, okay? It's been eating at me all week, and I wanted to tell you. I told her not to say anything. I wanted to be the one to tell you."

I swing at him again, but and it doesn't connect, and I scream out at him.

"Jace, stop."

He isn't fighting back. Why isn't he fighting me? I want to kill him.

I can't believe he would do that, that she would do that. Kiss him back. Unless she likes him?

She didn't say anything. They've been sitting beside each other all afternoon, giggling and poking each other. I'd assumed it was friendly banter, like siblings do. He always called her an annoying little sister. When the fuck did he go from thinking of her as a sister to kissing her?

I don't hear or see my parents as my fist connects with Grady's nose. My dad is the one to pull me from Grady, but I'm still seething.

"I wanted to tell you, because as amazing as it felt to

kiss her, the guilts been eating away at me. She was yours first. She won't ever be mine. I know that."

"Boys," Mom cries out.

Dad lets go of me; I think he knows I need to be alone. I storm into my room just as Dad calls out that I'm grounded. I slam the door and don't care if I'm grounded.

All I care about is whether she kissed my brother back.

Jace: Did Grady kiss you?

Mila: He told you?

Tears prick at my eyes, and I slump down to the floor.

Jace: Did you kiss him back?

She's typing, the three dots keep appearing as I wait for her answer.

Mila: Yes.

Three little letters, and my heart shatters.

THIRTY-ONE
ROMAN

The trailer smells like stale beer, tobacco, and body odor.

"Where you been, boy?"

I tense at my father's words. If you can even call him that. Sperm donor is what he is. Fucking waste of a human. It makes me sick that this is the man my mother married. Was he always like this? Fuck, I can't remember that far back, but when Mom was sick...I remember the way he put his hands on her and me. She was weak from all the chemo; she fought for a long time.

Fuck. I run my hand over my face. I don't want to think of Mom like that.

"Out," is all I give him. I don't tell him shit. He doesn't care where I've been as long as I bring money back to pay the rent and keep the power on.

He would notice if I died, of course, but only because the lights would go out, an eviction notice stuck to the front door.

I move toward my room at the back of the trailer, but he grabs my wrist as I pass, stopping me. I shake out of his grasp. "Fuck off," I mutter under my breath. I'm not in the mood for his shit tonight.

"Rent's due. Billy came looking for it earlier. I said he gotta wait till you get back." He looks up at me like I give a shit.

"Get a job." I roll my neck and it cracks, but he doesn't blink. He just stares at me like the lazy fuck he is.

"I'll fucking get it." I storm down to my room. I'm the child here. Not him. Yet, everything is paid for by me. I keep the roof over our heads. I keep food in the kitchen. He never cleans or cooks. I open my door and just stare at what used to be my room.

Everything been tossed out of the drawers. I'm not neat, but my room never looks like this. "What the fuck?" I roar to the shit stain in the living room. I go to where I stash the money for rent, and it's all gone.

"You fucking stole it." I screams as I stomp to him, and he just smiles like this is the funniest shit on earth.

"Nah, I borrowed some. Since you weren't back, I couldn't ask ya, now could I?"

The end of his cigarette glows orange as he inhales the tobacco. My fists ball up, and I'm ready to smash his face in.

"What. Did. You. Do?" I grit out between my clenched jaw.

He lays his head back on the dirty rotten armchair. "In me veins, and it felt so good." He scratches at his arm, and he leans forward, waving at me to come closer.

If I come any closer, I'm gonna smash his skull in.

"Don't happen to have more cash on ya, kid? I know you do good work down at The Shed. I told my dealer about ya. He gave me some extra smack on loan, cause he knows how good ya are. Says he seen you fight."

I take a deep breath and shake out my hand. *Two more years*. Just two more fucking years, and I'm out. I look at a faded photo of Mom and me hanging on the wall. The only one that hasn't been ripped up by the old prick.

"You know that's all I had, old man. We'll be evicted." The foster system will come get me. I'll end up in some group home far from here, and that can't happen. "And don't talk about me to your dealers. I have nothing to do with you."

No one loans a junkie smack without wanting something in return. And I can tell he has used my name to score more. Just another thing I have to fucking worry about.

I don't tell him that I have more cash. I have it stored somewhere safe. Somewhere he can't find. This isn't the first time he's shot rent money into his arm, and I know it won't be the last.

"Fucking junkie," I mutter under my breath as I walk away from him.

I look down at my phone to check the time. Saturday night is the best night at The Shed to make money. I march down to my room, flip my mattress up and back into its spot for later when I need to drop on it and sleep away the pain. I grab a towel and extra clothes and jam them in my bag before marching out, slamming the door behind me.

He doesn't hit me anymore. Not since I got bigger, and I hit twice as hard back. But this…I let out a deep breath. That money was for rent, and he knew it. He doesn't work. He never could keep a job, even when Mom was around.

I start up my Harley, the one thing that's mine. I worked hard, broke bones, for this baby. I throw my leather cut on; it says "prospect." But one day, it's gonna say "The Sons of Death MC." I've been prospecting with them for only a month. I met them through The Shed. They have a few guys down there that get in the ring and fight.

I see how they treat each other. Like family. They all have each other's backs, and I respect that. I know, with Hunter off to some fancy college across the country, and Jace waiting for a great college to offer him a place on their team and scholarship, I will still be here. *Alone.* If I choose to stay, I will become a full member of the MC. I will have family here. One I chose.

I won't hold Hunter and Jace back with them worrying about me. I want them to live their lives to the fullest. Take every opportunity that comes their way. I'm glad they have dreams, but I have this…a deadbeat dad. As soon as I turn eighteen, I'm out of there. Fuck, I don't know if I will even stay here in Ridgecrest. I live on the edge of town. The side you don't walk the streets at night if you're smart enough. Full of crack heads and junkies. Like my dad.

I might leave Ridgecrest. Find a new place to call my own. Ronnie has been teaching me all the skills I need to tattoo, and he says I can work with him at the shop full time when I'm done with school. He wants to retire and live a little by finally traveling. He knows about the MC, and he understands why. He didn't try talk me out of it. Not like Hunter or Jace would. They would worry and not want to leave if they knew my plans. That's why I haven't told them, and I don't ever intend on telling them. Ronnie also knows I might not stick around. He's cool with that. He's a good guy, says he only wants the best for me.

Doesn't take long to get to The Shed. It's not a shed but an old warehouse. These fights are illegal, but the cops turn a blind eye with a little cash handout every night.

It's packed as I walk in, men all sardined in and drunk

on beer and the sight of blood. Taylor's on door duty tonight.

"You fighting?" he asks, and I nod.

I need a decent fight, one that I can bring in at least six hundred. He shows me the roster.

"Fuck, Valentine's in The Shed tonight," a drunk guy calls out from the bar area. I'm greeted by some regulars as I look over to find the name I'm looking for.

Danny Holtz.

I beat him the last five time we fought, but the thing is, every time I fight him, I've taken weeks to recover. He's a tough son of a bitch. But I can't just do easy tonight. Rent's due. It's go in and go hard. Tonight.

I point to his name, and Taylor shakes his head.

"I love you, kid. You're a tough son of a bitch. But Holtz? During football season?"

"I need the cash. Dad fucking spent the rent money," I mutter. I don't like talking about him, but Taylor knows about my dad. I've been coming here for years. I started out in the bar, helping Arthur, and when I built up enough muscle, I was allowed into the ring.

"How much you need?"

"Six hundred."

He lets out a whistle. "Fucking prick. If I could take you in, kid, I would. No government gonna give me a kid, though."

He lets out a sigh and looks back at the board. There are a few names on there, ready to claim a fight. Taylor looks down at his sheet of paper. Scribbled numbers and the names are almost illegible, but I see the "2k" next to Danny Holtz. I know the quickest way of fixing my money problem is by fighting Holtz. I don't want to touch my savings.

"You can get your cash in an easier, less brutal way for your body. Don't have to destroy yourself. You could do a few of the newer guys, make it up that way. I have two coming up in the next hour. New kids. A hundred each, if you win. That's a good start to your rent problem."

The thing is, after what Dad said about his dealer knowing I'm down here, I'm worried they're gonna ask me for the cash he owes them. Drugs they loaned him. I don't know what that shit's about, but I also don't wanna find out. I want to be able to cover his debt and get them far away from me.

"Holtz."

Taylor throws his arms up. "Your funeral, kid."

I move over to the bar. I'm gonna need a shot of whisky before this goes down. Helps numb the pain a little.

approach the ring in the middle of the warehouse. Cheers go up when they see who's up next. Money's exchanging hands at a fast rate when they see me get into the ring. Holtz is on the other side. He has a trainer, someone to give a shit about him. I might be a prospect for The Sons of Death, but I have always worked alone.

The only times Jace or Hunter come here is when Arthur calls them, and I hope he hasn't called them tonight. I don't want to face them right now. One of them is gonna get Mila. One of them, meaning not me, and it's hard to sit back and watch.

I know I can't have her, *fuck*. When she said that shit last night about butterflies, I wished so hard for a different life. Any life outside of this shit so I could walk over to her and claim her. Kiss her again and tell everyone she's mine.

But I can't do that. She deserves someone like Jace or Hunter. They will give her a good life.

I'm not even paying attention when I put my mouth-guard in, and the ref is calling out if I'm ready.

Fuck, here we go.

Holtz bounces on his feet, zigzagging as he plays with me. Putting on a show is what he does best. His name might be Danny Holtz, but around here, he's known as "the Destroyer" because that's what he does. He doesn't just fight. He destroys his opponents.

I just want this shit to be over with. As Holtz dances, getting the crowd riled up, I make my move. I move in with a blow to the cheek. His head whips back around; fucker didn't see me until it's too late. I move back, bouncing lightly on my feet, ready for his move.

He rushes me, going for the face. I block and swing at him again. I catch his chin, but I'm not quick enough, and he catches my nose. The taste of blood fills my mouth before I feel it run down my face.

The crowd screams and cheers. They're out for blood tonight, and they'll have it. Only I'll be walking out of here two grand richer. And Holtz will be spread out on the mat.

I circle him, giving a good show as I throw out some feelers, see if he will bite. He does. I step to the right and let a powerful right hook send him reeling. I'm on him before he can think straight and smash his nose in. I hear the crack as it breaks under my fist. A few jabs to the ribs before he's on me, a sweep of my legs, and he takes me down.

This isn't your regular fighting. This shit is anything goes, as long as you only use your body. Holtz kicks my ribs, and my air whooshes out. I felt them crack. Fucker, they'd only just healed.

I try to breath in, but the pain is bad. Hell, he might have pierced my lung with that kick. I suck in what air I can, and I spin my legs around, taking him down before jumping up. The pain in my side causes white spots in my vision. But I take my chance while he's down, slamming my fist into his face, over and over. The blood. There's so much that I'm slipping in it.

"Stop, enough," I hear someone say, but I'm not thinking straight. I need to win, I need this. *I need it.*

"Roman."

My head snaps up at the sound of my name. Arthur is there. Fuck. He doesn't get in the ring unless he needs to step in.

I look down at Holtz. He's groaning, which is a good sign, but his face is unrecognizable.

Fuck, this is why I hate this shit. I hate who I've become. How could Mila ever want someone like me? If she saw this, she would be disgusted instead of getting butterflies. She wouldn't look at me the same. No more braids and lunches together. This is why she needs to stay far away from me.

I'm broken, and she can't fix me. No matter how hard she tries.

Arthur says he'll keep my Harley here overnight, secure. And one of the new guys, Brady, is gonna give me a lift back home.

I'm not sure if I've broken my fingers or if it's my knuckles. My hand doesn't seem to grip too well, and it's swollen as fuck from smashing Holtz's face in. It's lucky we have a bye week this Friday. The Rebels could win without me—Hunter is unbelievable right now—but I wouldn't have gone this far if I had a game on Friday. I wouldn't do that to the team and the guys.

I make my way through the crowd, who have long forgotten about me and are cheering on the next fighters of the night. There're hundreds of bodies packed in here, and I just want to leave, my two grand in my pocket.

"Hey, Valentine, been meaning to catch up with you."

I look over and find three thugs. "Your daddy tell you we were coming tonight?"

These aren't just any regular smack dealers; these guys are from the Amato family. Fuck's sake, Dad. What have you got me into? Since when does the mafia sell heroin to junkies like my dad? Or spend time down in The Shed?

"Yeah, he said if we want to collect his debt, we need to find you," the older one says.

"How much does he owe?" I stand straighter. I'm taller then all these fuckers. But I can see the guns holstered, so no matter our sizes, they are gonna win any fight with a bullet.

"Five. But we have a better deal."

Fuck's sake, I don't wanna give them five hundred. I'm dripping blood from my nose and hands. I just want to go home and sleep this shit off. But I don't want their better deal. There's no such thing as a better deal with these guys.

"Get it from him." I spit blood down at his feet.

"Nah, he said we get it from you. So, we get it from you. Or we break your legs."

The other snickers. "Bit hard chasing after a football with broken legs. End your football career."

They know who I am. They've done their research. This is why I can't have Mila. This right here is the reason I can't open up and let her in. I can't let anyone find a weakness. And Mila…she's my weakness. I would do anything for her. I would give my life for her. I need to make sure I stay away from her so these assholes don't see her and use her against me.

I hold five hundred dollar bills out to them, and the older one just stares at it. "Five grand."

My heart drops. Five grand? How the fuck did he rack up that much debt?

"Don't worry. We've seen you fight. We have a deal we wanna work out with you."

I don't like the sound of that. I'll get them the five grand. I'll fight more. It will take time, but I will get it for them. The three of them follow me out of the warehouse, and I tell Brady to wait for me near the entrance. They got a deal for me, and I don't think they're gonna let me leave until I hear it.

"You fight against Holtz again on Friday. But you lose. Make it look good. We know you're unmatched against him, won all six fights. We bet hard for Holtz to win. We take our winnings, and you get to pay off dear old daddy's debt."

"I'll get you the five grand, just give me a few weeks."

"We won't accept your cash. It's a done deal. See you Friday at midnight."

Fuck, fuck. Why can't just one thing go in my favor?

THIRTY-TWO
MILA

Jace didn't return any of my texts or answer his phone all of Sunday. His car wasn't there either. I know he's mad about the kiss with Grady. I'm a little upset that Grady didn't give me a head up. I told him as much this morning when he gave me a lift to school.

I'm supposed to be having dinner at their house tonight, but I can't with Jace not talking to me. I told Ella that something came up; I can't make it. She was sad, and I felt guilty. But I need to fix what's happened with Jace and me. He won't even let me explain that the kiss didn't mean anything. I don't feel that way about Grady.

"Hey, what's up with Jace this morning?" Hunter greets me, putting his arm around my shoulder and grinning down at me. At least he's not upset with me. Well, maybe he will be.

"I kissed Grady last week. Jace found out Saturday, and now he won't talk to me."

Hunter blinks a few times, as if he's trying to register what I just said. He's so cute right now. "You kissed Grady?" His puzzled expression has me laughing.

"Why's it so hard to believe that he kissed me?"

He shrugs. "Nah, I just thought…huh? So, Grady? Was he a good kisser?"

Hunter's playful banter has me smiling. I love this. I'm upset that Jace doesn't want to be part of it. Hell, Friday was amazing, and I'm upset that nothing happened. But now to stop talking to me without even letting me explain?

"Did he give you butterflies?" he whispers into my ear. His hot breath tickles my neck just before he pulls back to study my face.

"No. Not like you do."

I smile to myself as his warm body presses close to mine. I love his warmth, his strength, against me like that. I look up at him under my lashes, and he bites his lip, groaning as he rolls his eyes back dramatically. I smack his chest, and he bursts out laughing.

"I'm glad. I was thinking, fuck, another contender. I can't be responsible for all the heartbreak here when I make you mine."

I laugh. Hunter can always pick me up and make me feel better. But the butterflies in my tummy tell me I want him to make me his. But it's not right, not while Jace is upset with me. I need to fix that before I can move forward with anyone right now.

Hunter walks me to chemistry. Great. I will have to see Jace, and I don't want him to say something hurtful. I just can't take it right now. I got my period this morning, so I'm a little crampy and hormonal. And I might burst into tears if he is mean. I'm allowed to have a sad, sulky day now and then, and today is looking like that day.

I walk in, ignoring where Jace is, and sit beside Roman.

"Hey, how was your weekend?"

He just nods and doesn't speak. Shit, is he upset with

me because of Grady too? God, I wish that kiss hadn't happened. But at least I know I don't feel the same way about Grady as I used to. Sometimes, a crush should be left in the past. The spark isn't there. But it is with Hunter, Jace, and my quiet Roman.

I notice his hands are bandaged.

"Shit, are you okay? Did you get into a fight with your dad?"

He shakes his head as he pulls his hands away from the table so I can't see them anymore. Fuck. That's not good. How is he gonna play football with his hands like that? At least there a bye this week. But will he be ready next week?

"You ready for our study session tomorrow?" I ask, trying to change the subject.

He looks at me now, but it's as if he isn't seeing me. Rather, he's looking through me. His breathing quickens, and I notice his body trembling. What did I say wrong? Oh, god, Roman.

"No, I can't study with you anymore."

And, in the blink of an eye, he's back to staring ahead. His body is still and breathing normal. What the hell just happened?

"Is it the conversation from Friday? I know you don't see me that way. It's fine. I just wanted you to—"

"No," he cuts me off. His voice is low and deep, but I hear the warning in it not to push him.

And I won't. I swallow the lump in my throat. I knew he didn't want to kiss me again, that he didn't want anything else with me, but I thought we were becoming friends. It's been a slow start, but we'd made progress. At least, I thought we had.

· · ·

L unch comes, and I make my way outside, but Roman isn't there. I let out a breath and look to the sky. "Fuck," I mutter to myself. This is worse than I thought.

"Yeah, fuck."

I turn just in time to see chocolate milk flying through the air. It hits me, dripping down my face and hair. I stand there, my mouth open in shock as I look over at Britney, who has her hand covering her mouth to stifle her laugh.

"Oh gosh, I tripped with my milk bottle open. It was an accident."

I lick my lips and the chocolatey flavor hits my taste buds. Summer snickers from beside her and takes a photo. I put my food down on the ground and shake my hair and clothes. Fuck, this is gonna smell bad with the heat today.

There are a bunch of students around, some are laughing, some staring. And I realize I didn't bring my spare clothes today. I forgot in my rush to get to school and confront Jace, which didn't happen, anyway.

"Shit, Mila." Hunter comes running over. He looks to me then to Britney. "You threw your milk on her? God, how old are you? Six?"

Hunter is mad. I can't fight Britney here. There're too many eyes and cameras. I just smile and run a finger down my cheek and lick it.

"Mmm…sorry you wasted your milk. Tastes great."

Britney snickers and calls me a whore under her breath. I ignore her as I let Hunter lead me past the crowd that's gathered to see what's happening and to my locker.

"I would give you something from my gym bag. But, yeah…" He scratches the back of his neck.

I scrunch my nose up at him. "You haven't washed anything in there?"

He shrugs and gives me a goofy grin.

"Hunter, you need to wash those things. Chances are, things are growing in there. At least throw out the old food." I grab my bag from my locker, I can't stay here. Not like this.

"Do you want me to give you a lift home?" he asks, and I give him my best *I'm okay* smile.

"Please. I need a shower."

I text Dad to let him know and sign myself out. The pitying looks from the office staff don't help my souring mood at all.

The drive back to my house is filled with silence. I don't want to talk about it. It's been a weird day, and I need some time alone to process it. Jace isn't talking to me, Roman seems angry at me, and Britney got me...finally. Wasn't expecting milk, I'll give her that.

The only one talking to me right now is Hunter, and I'm grateful for that. He doesn't know how much I need him right now.

"I'll stay if you want me to. But I gotta get to practice later."

"No, go. I'll be fine. I think a bath might do me good, anyway. I have some bad cramps."

Hunter stares at me like I grew two heads. Oh, god, what's with boys acting weird around girls with their periods?

"You have your period?"

I nod.

He cocks his head and smirks. "You want my shorts?"

I hold my belly and let out the biggest laugh of the day. The memories of that day at the lake flood in, and I hug Hunter as best I can without getting the sticky milk on him.

"God, that was an interesting day…and a more interesting first kiss. You're the only one who took his shorts off."

He laughs harder now, and I can't stop myself either. It's funny.

"Well, they didn't know how to do a first kiss right. Shorts off is the best way to kiss."

We finally stop laughing, and he pulls back to look down at me. His big brown eyes search my face as he gives me a sweet smile and kisses my forehead.

"If you need anything, call me, and I'll grab it for you. Chocolate, ice cream, tampons. You name it, I'll get it for you."

"Thank you." I choke back tears. He's being so perfect right now, and my head is too fucked up to ask him to stay. I need to relax and think about how I'm goin to approach Jace over all this. And plotting how to get Britney back is something fun to do while in the bath.

I let out a deep breath and turn to the bathroom. I don't turn the water on until I hear him close the front door behind him. Then I let out the tears.

t's late and dark when I'm woken by the buzzing sound of the walkie-talkie.

Jace? I rub my eyes and look over to my windowsill. I hear something coming through. Is he trying to talk to me? I check my phone; it's after midnight.

I move to my window and open the curtains, trying to see over to his room, but it's dark. Maybe my walkie-talkie is picking up someone else talking? The sounds coming through aren't clear. But then I hear a moan and "oh yeah."

That voice is clearly Jace's. Is he jerking off in his room and broadcasting it to me? That's not how I thought he would want to talk to me again, but I'll pay along if it means he's talking to me. I bring the walkie-talkie up to my mouth...

"Oh, Britney," he says, and I freeze, looking down at it in my hand. He...what? Britney. I look over to his room. The blind is clearly open, but it's dark in there. I can't see anything. My nose is pressed so close to the glass of my window, I can feel the chill in the air outside.

Suddenly, his room lights up, and I see him standing fully naked at the end of his bed, his hand is wrapped around hair. The hair is attached to the girl on his bed on all fours, sucking on his cock.

Britney Montlake.

His eyes meet mine, and I feel like I've been slapped as I shuffle back in shock. I watch as he moves his hand closer to where her mouth is wrapped around his hard length. She is bobbing up and down, and his hips move in time.

Slurping sounds come through on my end, and I throw the walkie-talkie across my room like it burned me.

"Oh, god, Britney."

The sound echoes around my room as I scramble down to stop it before my dad walks in to see what's happening. When I threw it, the volume dial must have increased to max.

All I can hear is them...

"Just like that, god, you know how I like it."

I want to vomit.

Why? Why would he do that? To get back at me over the kiss?

I close my curtains and rip the batteries out of the walkie- talkie. I never want to use them again. He has tarnished something that held such great memories from our childhood.

I hate Jace Montero.

THIRTY-THREE
MILA

I don't go to school all week.

Dad's worried, so much that he makes me talk to Kate on Wednesday. I tell her I have my period; my cramps are worse than usual, and I have been so run down, I think I have a cold coming on. I just need to rest, and I'll be fine soon.

She's sweet and tells Dad I'm fine. But she also tells me that, when I'm ready, she's there to talk. But if I don't talk to her, I should talk to someone. I love that she notices I'm not okay. My own mother, who still hadn't spoken to me since I left, wouldn't have seen this. She would have said, "Get up, get over it. Cramps are normal."

"I've seen you getting close with Asher. If you want to talk to him, I can ask him to come over."

Ugh...Asher isn't going to help me. He would probably just go put his fist into Jace's nose, and I can't have that on my conscience. He has a game tonight, and Dad asked me to come. Asher texted me and told me he has a blue jersey waiting for me. But I couldn't make myself go.

Hunter has been over every day. He's been really

worried about me, and just like he said, he brought me chocolate, ice-cream, and tampons...six different boxes because he didn't know which ones I liked. I never asked for any of it; he took it upon himself to do that for me.

He has cheered me up, but when he asks what's wrong, I don't know how to tell him. He's best friends with Jace and has been saying all week that "Jace will come around. He's just being moody and shit."

But where do I even go from here?

I have only ever felt like this once before...the weeks after Mom dragged me to live with her, and I missed my friends so much that I cried for three weeks.

Sleeping, sad movies, and chocolate have gotten me through this week, and I have ignored every one of Hunter's calls to me tonight.

There's a party somewhere, and he probably wants me to go.

I roll over, hug my old teddy bear to my chest, and stare at my laptop. It's playing *P.S I Love You* for the tenth time this week. My eyes are raw from all the tears, but this movie, it just gets me every time. If I want to cry, all I have to do is look at the name of the movie, and the tears start to flow. Hell, maybe I should move to Hollywood and become an actress with how fast and easy I can cry to this movie.

My door slams open, and I gasp, scrambling from my bed. I get caught in my sheets and land with a thud on the floor. My heart races—someone's in my room. Someone broke into my house. I panic, trying to find a weapon, but all I have is my sketch pads and a pencil beside me. I reach out and grip the pencil tightly, holding it out in front of me to stop whoever is in my room.

"Mila?"

"Hunter?" I look over my bed to Hunter, who looks worried.

"I called you on your phone and you didn't pick up. And I've been calling out to you from downstairs."

I press my hand to my chest to stop my heart form racing and try to even out my breathing. "Holy shit, Hunter." I take a deep breath and slowly let it out while he watches what I'm doing. "You gave me a heart attack."

"Shit, I'm sorry about that, but Roman's in trouble. I need your help to get through to him. He's gonna fight at The Shed tonight, and he's still got broken ribs and his hand isn't looking great either.

"I think it's infected, but he won't go get it checked out. He looks like shit. I need you to come with me. I think you're the only one who can get through to him."

I scramble up to my feet and rush to my closet, throwing on a pair of jeans and a hoodie over my sports bra. I don't have time; we need to get Roman. God, I'll be so devastated if he's hurt because I didn't answer Hunter's calls.

I'd crawled into a deep, dark hole this week and forgotten about Roman. How he'd acted so different on Monday, pushing me away. All this week, I have sobbed and eaten my weight in chocolate while he's been fighting his own inner demons, needing someone there to chase them away.

That person's gonna be me.

🏈 🏈 🏈

The Shed is huge. I've heard about it before; it's one of those places you hear about in a story. You don't go there.

Men outnumber women here, like a hundred to one. For something underground and illegal, it's set up well. There is standing room, and the stands surround all four sides of the ring in the middle of the floor.

Hunter keeps me close to his side, and I'm grateful. The way men leer scares me. Hunter isn't strong enough to protect me from all of them.

"We need to find Roman or Arthur. He called me, told me I need to come down and talk him out of the fight," Hunter yells over the men cheering.

They were cheering on two men fighting. I gasp, and cold chills run though my body. That tattoo…on his chest. A daisy. My Daisy. Hunter tries to pull me, but my hand is covering my mouth, and I can't speak.

Roman's face is covered in so much blood, it's unrecognizable. Hunter finally looks over and see's what I do. When we first looked over, I wouldn't have known it was him. The other guy is landing blow after blow.

"Fuck, fuck, where's Jace when all this is going down? Fuck's sake." Hunter pulls me through the screaming crowd; they're not happy that we're pushing in front of them. A few shove Hunter, but he just keeps on pushing through and dragging me behind.

We get to the edge of the ring, and I can tell that one of Roman's eyes is swollen shut.

"Shit, I've never seen him like this," Hunter croaks. "Ever."

I scream when the other guy lands a blow to Roman's face and he drops to one knee. I'm shaking and numb. I don't know much about this type of fighting, but can't he tap out?

"Tap out already, stop," I call out to him, and his one good eye meets mine just as a knee jams into his side and he lets out a painful groan.

"Roman, stop," Hunter calls out. He's moving away from me, leaving me on the side to watch this alone. "Roman," Hunter yells from the corner of the ring, and Roman looks over at him now, spitting blood on the mat.

I feel an arm come around my shoulder, and I flinch away, but it doesn't help. The man holds me even closer.

"Ah, what do we have here…a little angel come to see her boy beaten?"

I look at the man. His eyes are wild, and I try to push away from him, but another man grips my chin and turns me to face him.

"Call out all you want. We own your boy right now, and you can say nighty night to him." His finger digs into my chin as Roman looks over at me now. His eye flares with something wild, and he lets out a guttural cry.

God, Roman. What have they done to you?

He charge toward me, but the other guy in the ring appears in front of him. All I see is a spray of blood. It hits me, covering my hair and face. It's the same for the two men beside me as Roman's opponent hits the mat right in front of me and lets out a small moan before closing his eyes and going limp.

Holy fuck. Roman just knocked him out.

The guys beside me roar out in anger. Roman doesn't stop; he steps over the guy laying there, bleeding out while the ref is trying to wake him, and he reaches down over the rope, grabs the scruff of the hoddie I'm wearing, and hauls me up and over the rope and into the ring.

"Roman, oh god," I cry, my hands reaching out, wanting to touch him but not even knowing where to start that isn't already bruised or broken.

He doesn't look at me. He just carries me over to where Hunter is now beside Jace. I don't have time to think about that. Roman's injured, and he needs a hospital.

"Why did you bring her? I said to never bring her here," he yells at Hunter.

Roman shoves me at Hunter and I turn, reaching out to Roman. He just spins and walks to the other side of the ring. My voice cracks as I call out his name, but he doesn't turn around. He leaves the ring and me.

"What just happened?" I demand from Hunter as soon as I'm wrapped up in his arms.

He shakes his head and looks over to where Roman had walked away.

"I don't know."

◀▥▶ ◀▥▶ ◀▥▶

I don't sleep at all. I can't. Hunter has been out all night, looking for Roman. No one has seen him, and I'm worried something bad has happened. Like, he went to sleep and is so injured that he passed out and is bleeding to death.

My stomach won't settle as I pace my room, biting my nails and thinking of all the bad things that could have happened.

Mila: did you try his dad again?

Hunter: yes, he hasn't seen him.

Mila: the lake?

I'm grasping at straws here.

Hunter: tried there, Arthur is out looking for him too.

I can't sit here, but I don't have a car. Dad stayed over at Kate's last night. He has no idea what's going on, and I don't want to tell him. Not yet. I don't want him looking at Roman differently because of this.

His mom? Would he go visit his mom? Shit, why didn't I think of that earlier?

I run down the stairs two at a time, shove my feet into my trainers, and run out to the shed. My old bike is there. It's pink and covered in cobwebs. I pull it out, making a racket as I do. I place it down in front of me and test out the tires. They're all good. I jump on and wobble a little. But I start to pedal, and it all comes back to me.

"Like riding a bike." I smile to myself.

But then I remember why I'm on the bike. I let out a deep, shuddering breath and make my way to the cemetery to see if Jeanie Valentine knows where her son is.

My chest burns and my legs feel like jelly as I ride into the cemetery. It's big, but I know exactly where she is. As I get closer, I can see that he's not here, and my heart sinks. I'd been hoping he would be. I see a daisy bush not too far away and jog over and pick five flowers off of it. I smile down at them. Roman and I would pick them once a week when we visited here.

I make my way over to Jeanie and kneel at her headstone.

"Hey, Jeanie, it's been a long time since I've been here, and I apologize. I should have come sooner and under different circumstances. But I'm here now, and I need your help." I place the flowers on top of her headstone and smile.

"Have you seen Roman? I bet you have. If you could tell me where he is, give me a sign, I would be forever grateful. I don't want to sound rude, but I don't want him visiting you just yet. I want to keep here with me a lot longer. So, if you see him up there, tell him to come back to me. He can't stay with you. I'll miss him too much." A tear slips from my face.

My phone buzzes in my pocket.

Hunter's calling me. I answer. "You find him?"

"No, where are you?" he asks.

"I'm visiting his mom. I hoped he came here, so I rode over on my bike."

"I'm at your place. Do you want me to come get you?"

"No, my bike will mess up your car. I'll meet you at mine. We can go out and look for him together."

"Okay, I'll see in you in twenty."

I hang up and put my phone back in my pocket.

"Promise me you won't keep him if he come to you, Jeanie." I kiss my fingers and press them against the cold, hard stone then stand. I walk over to my bike and start my way back home.

"Give me a sign," I call out to the sky, pedaling as fast as I can to meet Hunter. Every minute we're not looking is another minute that Roman could be dying somewhere. And time seems to be against us today.

I'm about five minutes into my ride when I hear a car pull up beside me. I look over; it's black and shiny but not Jace's car. The window glides down, and a face I recognize from last night is behind the wheel.

"Well, hello there, angel."

THIRTY-FOUR
ROMAN

They kept me locked up for hours, beating the shit out of me until I passed out. Over and over, they told me I failed them, as if I didn't already know that. They're out fifty grand because of my stunt last night.

They touched Mila, and I lost control. I had to put on a good show, so no one would think I threw the fight. But when they touched her, something came over me. I couldn't see anything but her being touched by them, and I wanted them dead. The assholes dumped me at the cemetery.

To "show me where I will be buried with my girl."

Mila's on their radar now. They said if I don't give them fifty grand, they'll kill her. Everything's fucked. *I fucked up.* But Mom has the money. She has it there, stored away safely. It's not fifty grand, but I can ask Hunter or Jace for a loan. I have to keep Mila safe. If anything happens to her, I will never forgive myself.

I drag my broken body down to Mom.

I let out a strangled sob when I see her name and reach

out to trace it, leaving a smear of blood where the gold of the J once was.

"Mom, god. I need you." I lay my head down on the grass. I need to close my eyes, just for a moment.

"Whenever you need me, I will be right here. Watching, looking down from heaven. I will give you a sign. Look for them." I choke back a sob. Mom is so frail, her face is so thin I can see all the bones. It scares me.

"I don't have anyone to love me when you go." The tears stream down my face now.

"You have Mila. She's a good friend and I know you'll grow up to be a strong, brave man."

"I'm gonna marry her mom." I try to smile, I don't want her to see me sad.

"Make sure you protect her, she might seem strong and brave all the time. But she's human just like you and me." Mom's hand is cold as she touches my cheek.

"I promise Mom, I will take care of Mila. She can count on me to keep her safe."

The breeze picks up, and it feels good on my hot body. Something lands on my face, and I brush it away. When the breeze picks up again, it happens for a second time. This time, I pick it off my face and pull it back to see with my eye, the one not swollen shut.

A daisy? Where did that come from? I look beside me and see another, the first one that fell on me. I push myself up and look at Mom. Is she sending me daisies? Is this a sign?

But then I see three more perched on the top of the headstone. I reach out and take one. These have been freshly picked and placed here only recently.

I hear the crunch of metal, and a scream rips through the air. My stomach drops. I look to the road before turning back to the daisies as they all fall to the ground and scatter in the breeze.

Oh god. *Mila.*

With every ounce of energy I have left, I run to her.

"Mila?" I call out, stumbling.

My ribs are broken, and every breath I take makes my body scream in pain. I need to get to her, so I press on as fast as I can, the white spots dancing in my vision with every breath I take.

My throat is hoarse and doesn't carry far. "Mila?" I call again once I make it to the narrow street in front of the cemetery.

"Mila?" My throat feels like it's closing as my vision swims.

Lying on the road is a small figure and a mangled pink bike.

Oh, god, Mila.

My feet stumble, one after the other, trying to get to her. But I feel like I'm wading through water, my body going backward. This is a nightmare; one I can't escape.

"Mila?" God, answer me, tell me you're alive.

"Roman?" her small voice carries to me.

I stumble and land beside her head, my hands hovering over her body. Blood pours from a gash on her head, her blonde hair now as red as the jersey I wear every Friday night. I don't know where to touch her, where to begin to help.

"Help," I cry out. "Somebody help?"

I don't have my phone, so I can't call nine-one-one.

"Roman, you're safe. I found you." She chokes out a

sob, her big blue eyes peering up at me. I brush her hair away from her eyes, so she can see me better.

"I'm safe. You found me," I whisper to her. She's going to be okay. She's strong, my beautiful Mila.

She coughs and groans. Oh, god. Blood trickles from her mouth, and I wipe it away with my thumb, as if that small act will make it all go away. As if she doesn't have internal bleeding.

I cradle her head in my hands. "Keep looking at me. Don't close your eyes."

A woman calls out, and I turn to her. She yells to me that she's got help on the way.

I turn back to Mila. "Hear that? Help's on the way. They will come fix you up. You just gotta keep breathing. You have to stay with me, Mila."

"I'm cold."

Her body is trembling, and I don't have anything to cover her with. I have nothing but the shorts I wore for the fight last night.

"I got you. I'll keep you warm." She closes her eyes and my heart drops. "Mila, come on. Mila, open your eyes."

More blood trickles from her mouth, and I let out a cry, trying to wipe it away, but it's not stopping. I clean her face as best I can while I call her name, over and over again.

"Wake up," I cry out, and I'm rewarded with two blue eyes...and a small smile. I release a ragged breath.

"Don't do that to me, sweet girl. You scared me. I need to see your beautiful eyes. I need you here with me."

She tries to reach out to me, and I grab her hand and hold it. She's so cold. Fuck, this is really bad.

"I see you, Roman."

"Good, just stay with me. Help is on the way." I can hear sirens coming closer. They'll save her.

"Kiss me," she whispers.

"Just keep breathing. I will kiss you when you're safe."

"No, I need you to kiss me, Roman."

"Why?"

"Because you were my first. I want you to be my last."

I press my lips to hers, and she lets out a small sigh. I promise this won't be her last kiss. She's gonna be fine.

I pull back from her just as the red and blue lights start to dance across her face.

Her eyes flutter closed, and her body goes limp in my arms.

Fuck, no.

Mila.

GET THE LIE

Pre order Link here:

www.books2read.com/theliebelleharper

BELLE'S BOOKS

PARANORMAL REVERSE HAREM

NEW MOON SERIES ~LEXI~

Twice Bitten

Blood Moon

Rising Sun

FULL MOON SERIES ~ADA~

Fallen Wolf

Torn Mate

Shifting Sun

BLUE MOON SERIES ~ INDI~ COMING 2022

Rogue Wolf

Broken Mate

Indigo Dreams

PACK KIBA NOVELS/NOVELLAS

Midnight Prince

Shadow Wolf

Wolf Karma- Late 2022

SEEKING EDEN SERIES

Dystopian/ Post Apocalyptic Reverse Harem

Finding Nova

Protecting Nova

Rescuing Harlow

Claiming Harlow

BRIDES OF THE AASHI SERIES

Alien Romance RH

Luna Touched

Brooklyn's Baggage

Quinn Inspired

Jessica's Mates

Elle Embraced

Hadley's Heroes

REBELS OF RIDGECREST HIGH

Reverse Harem ~ Enemies to Lovers

The Pact

The Lie ~ Coming August

TBA ~ Coming October

TBA ~ Coming November

CONTEMPORARY STANDALONES

Naughty and Nice ~Christmas Novella

ABOUT THE AUTHOR

Belle is an Artist, Author, Wife and Mother.

She has an addiction to reading, notebooks, coloured pens and mint chocolate. She lives in the beautiful Australian bush, surrounded by wildlife and the smell of eucalyptus trees.

She also has a strong love for all 60's music, believes she was born in the wrong era and should have been at Woodstock.

If you would like to find out more about Belle, please come like and follow her:

Click Here to Like Belle's Facebook Page

Join Belle in her Facebook Group

Visit my website HERE

Sign up to my Newsletter to keep up to date with my new Releases, Free Books and Giveaways.

Sign Up HERE

Made in the USA
Columbia, SC
19 December 2023

29036783R00159